DARK HORSES

The Magazine of Weird Fiction

NOVEMBER | 2024

No. 34

Copyright © 2024 Hobb's End Press. All Rights Reserved. Published by Hobb's End Press, a division of ACME Sprockets & Visions. Cover design Copyright © 2024 Wayne Kyle Spitzer. All stories Copyright © 2024 by their respective authors. Please direct all inquiries to: HobbsEndBooks@yahoo.com

CONTENTS

THE WAREHOUSE AT WORLD'S END
Bill Link

COMPANION™, LOST
Nadim Silverman

THE FMMLADE
R.S. Morgan

I DON'T DO DRUGS: I AM A DRUG
Curt Tyler

FARAWAY, NEARBY
Wayne Kyle Spitzer

SIGN ON THE DOTTED LINE
David Sheskin

THE HOLE
Meg Keane

THE NUNNERY
Nathan Perrin

THE PRIESTS
Alexander Zelenyj

THICKER THAN WATER
Dylan T. Bosworth

THE WAREHOUSE AT WORLD'S END

A *Dead of Night* Story

Bill Link

Chapter 1

When the rasping voice coming over the phone identified itself as Viktor, the first thing Status Chelan thought was, how was it that this man, who had been old the last time they had spoken over thirty years ago, was still alive. The second thought he had concerning this old monster he spoke out loud: "How did you get this number?" He heard the tremor of fear in his own voice.

"I Googled it, like everybody these days." Viktor's old man cough was phlegmy. "I called because I wanted to make you a proposition."

"Who's on the phone?" Paula asked, walking into the kitchen where Status was seated at the pile of bills and past due notices heaped on the dinner table. Behind her, a purplish evening sky was visible through the window between redwood kitchen cabinets placed above the counter and sink. "It's not a bill collector, is it?" she whispered the question, seeing how his face had gone white, and his shoulders and back had gone rigid. Glancing quickly at her, he shook his head.

"Listen, I appreciate the offer," Status lied, feeling his mouth go dry. "But I'm really busy at the moment, so..."

"I'm well aware how our parting of the ways was far from amiable, Status, but you and AK were hardly the only ones who felt you got a raw deal out of it. I'm only assuming that's why you two skipped town without notice, leaving me in a lurch with no employees to take care of matters. And then to add insult to injury, I get your resignations in the mail!"

"What do you want? For me to tell you I'm sorry?" Status asked, feeling his patience already dwindling.

"I want bygones to be bygones." The old man's whispery voice paused to cough, again. "I've got a major job in the works for a particular client, and I need reliable security on site here in Grand Central that's... beyond the scope of talent and expertise that my current employees are capable of."

"I haven't talked to AK for years, now, so I can hardly speak for him. As for myself... I'm doing alright with my own security firm these days. So, my answer has to be no." With his finger about to press disconnect on the phone, he saw how Paula's eyes, widening with incredulity, looked as if they might roll out of her head.

"One hundred thousand, for single night's work."

"One hundred thousand?" He looked at the hopeless pile of envelopes on the table before him, when a moment later, he shook his head, remembering who this terrible old man was. "Again, no. Please don't call here, again."

"Don't delete my number," Viktor's tone of voice sounded like a warning, before Status hung up on him.

"So, why the need to shovel the horseshit about how *well* we're doing?" Paula asked, her hands resting on her hips, suspicion on her face. "And what's this about a hundred thousand?"

"An old boss from thirty years back," he said furtively, as he slumped in the chair behind the kitchen table. "He said he wanted to hire me back for a single night's work."

"For a hundred thousand dollars? And you turned him down? Did you forget about all the people we owe money to?" she demanded, pointing at the bills and notices he had been about to go through – again – and still finding there wasn't enough money in checking, or left on the credit cards, and not at all in savings where the balance was at zero, to pay it all. "Did you forget how we're about to lose everything we've spent years working for?"

"No, I haven't forgotten about any of that," he sighed, feeling defeated, propping his elbows on the table top to lower his head into his waiting hands. "It's all I ever think about, because it's all you talk about, anymore."

"Fuck you. Stop trying to make me the bad guy," she muttered bitterly, before she turned and walked back out into the living room.

No, he very well knew it wasn't the fault of the pretty woman of Japanese extraction, with her long, black hair and almond eyes, who he was in love with, and who he hoped was still in love with him. Fifteen years ago, Paula Ota and he had become partners in the company they had founded, *Dark Horse Security*, and soon after, they began sharing a bed together. Business had been good over the years, with the two even investing in the three storied house they had resided in for almost a decade. Then, Covid hit, and many of the businesses that had hired them to provide on-site security either went tits up, or could only make ends meet by cutting back on live guards in favor of alarm systems. Even the companies that stuck with them ended up renegotiating their contracts, paying much less for services. Even after letting half their staff go, both he and Paula knew it was only a matter of time till they, too, became casualties of the Covid 19 pandemic.

"I'm sorry. It's been tough for both of us." He felt Paula's hands rest gently on his shoulders from behind. "You said the call came from an old boss from thirty years ago," she said softly, feeling her breath against his ear, as she leaned close to him. "It's that blank spot in your life you asked me never to bring up, isn't it?"

He nodded with a listless frown as he sat up straight, letting his hands rest on the table. The cell phone rang, again. "Let voice mail pick it up," he said, when she reached for it. After all this time of bill collectors harassing them, and now hearing a voice he had long ago hoped he could forget, he knew they should fall into the habit of screening their calls from now on.

"I never asked you why you didn't want to talk about that time in your life. I just assumed you had been made to do something wrong. Maybe even illegal." She rubbed his shoulder blades, feeling how tense he had become. "I just wanted to let you know, whatever it was... it could never be so bad that I'd leave you for it, if that's what you've been afraid of."

Status had shared everything with this woman; even the embarrassing sexual misadventures of his youth. But he had never uttered a word about the years he spent working for Viktor. And what would he tell her? That he and his best friend had worked for that old man in the town of Grand Central, where the fabric of reality had worn so thin in places that walking nightmares could pass through into our place in time and space? Or how Viktor had hired the two of them to drive about the town in the small hours between twelve and two in the morning, keeping up with the random - and maybe not so random – portals or *fluxcores*, saving a blissfully ignorant humanity from the edge of damnation?

"If you want to tell me, I'll listen. No judgment." She brought her arms around his neck and pressed the side of her face gently against his. "If not now, then someday."

He chuckled, sadly. "Believe me, you'd have me committed. And I wouldn't blame you a damn bit."

"Then please, at least tell me who that man... I'm assuming it was a man... who called was."

"His name's Viktor, and he was an old man running a security company," Status began, slowly, choosing his words carefully before he spoke them out loud. "The things he had me and my friend, AK, do... we both thought was important. Most of the time, the information he gave us was on a need-to-know basis, leaving AK and me in the dark, which at the time, we thought was just irksome than anything else. He'd have us take things from the jobs we were involved with, which he hid away in some warehouse or other. Things most rational people would have thought were dangerous and would've considered untouchable. We just put on our big boy pants, because at the time we thought Viktor was on the side of the angels," he laughed humorlessly.

"But his motives weren't so pure, I'm assuming," her voice was so soft it was almost a whisper.

Status shook his head, his eyes down on the table top. "I began understanding Viktor had schemes within schemes, and whatever his motives were, they probably weren't meant to benefit anyone else in the long run. Then this new kid who got hired on... died."

"My God!" Standing up, Paula went to one of the other chair at the kitchen table, and sat down. "What happened?"

Status only shook his head again, as memories flickered behind his eyes like a movie reel. He couldn't even remember the young guy's name after all this time, barely even recalled what he looked like, save that he had been a new hire. What he had seen in that two hour period of chilly, early morning darkness had terrified him so much that he quit immediately after. It had been after dawn when AK and he had come upon the kid's wrecked automobile, and the body beneath a sheet being carried off by first responders. They had only wordlessly looked at one another, knowing this car accident wasn't an accident. Not when it came to that old man, who they had long ago come to realize how maybe nothing was beyond his capabilities. They both had to ask one another, if Viktor wasn't going to let an employee go after seeing the horror behind the curtain of reality after just one night, then what would he have in store for them eventually?

After withdrawing what money each had from the bank, and packing as quickly as possible, he and AK had blown out of town, both agreeing to send Viktor their resignations by mail, with no return address. After having gone their separate ways, Status had no idea if AK had made it out alive, in the end. He himself had spent the next five years living off the grid, working shit jobs under assumed names, and always, *ALWAYS*, looking over his shoulder. Eventually, he had gone back to using his real name, got credit cards again, started a business and fell in love, and even got a Facebook page after he had thought that old man couldn't still be alive. Until today, he had convinced himself he was out of Viktor's reach.

Status shook the cobwebs from his head, realizing he had been silent for several moments too long, lost in his own memories. "Car accident," he cleared his throat. "The kid died in a car accident. But it was enough for my friend and me to cut ties to that old bastard."

"I won't push it." She pursed her lips and laid her hand on his. "You can tell me when you're ready." Straightening, she rubbed his shoulders. "The only thing you've ever mentioned was your friend, AJ."

"AK," he corrected her, realizing he hadn't thought about his old friend for... what? Years? Now he did...

The hoot from out of the darkness caused Status to whirl around with a frightened gasp as his eyes searched the unseen tree branches beyond the apartment house' driveway. "It's just an owl, man," AK assured him. His dark face was caught in the stark light from the interior light shining from the open door of his pickup, which cast the shadow of his big frame across the road.

"Just an owl... yeah," Status tried to laugh it off.

"We're doing this for real, right?" Of the two of them, AK had always been the one ready to go in, fists flying to settle any problem, even if it had crawled out of the pit of Hell, but now for the first time, there was a look of uncertainty on the Latino man's face. This would be the last time either would see this town, or Viktor, again, even going to the extent of tossing their black security guard uniforms.

"If we want to stay alive, you know we gotta disappear." Status pursed his lips.

A moment later, both men squeezed one another in an embrace, knowing this would be the last time either would see the other. Status felt a moment's embarrassment as his eyes teared up, till he heard a sob escape his friend's throat. "Stay alive, man," Status' voice cracked as he quickly wiped his eyes, then turned and hurried to his car. Before driving away, he saw his friend standing in the light of his pickup's open door, his head of thick black hair and shoulders sadly slumped down.

Status cleared his throat. "Well, let's see who called," he said, eager to change the subject as he picked up the cell phone, and brought up voice mail.

"This is Herb Vascone from *Speedy Collections* calling for Status Chelan and Paula Otta," the disembodied voice barked from the phone. "Avoiding my calls isn't going to make the debt you incurred go away. Unless this matter is not resolved, legal action will..."

Status pressed erase before hanging up. Closing his eyes, his face dropped with a sigh: "How much do we owe those cocksuckers at *Speedy*, again?"

Paula shook her head with a frown. "Fifty thousand, I think. I'd have to look."

"God fucking damn it," he mumbled, his eyes still down on the phone. A moment later, he was scrolling through the recent calls, when he came to the number for *ViktorCorp*. Punching in redial, the voice in his head warned him, *Don't do this,* as he put the phone to his ear and listened to the ringing. "Shut up," he whispered to that inner voice, when he heard the phone pick up on the other end.

"I knew you'd call back," came the hoarse voice.

"I'll do it."

"Status... you don't have to do this," Paula whispered, shaking her head.

"I knew you'd come around, my boy!"

"But only if we can renegotiate the offer." Status eyed the pile of bills and final notices on the table.

The cackle over the other line ended in a feeble cough. "Of course. Go on."

Every one of your debts will be covered, on top of the one hundred thousand, Viktor had promised Status, along with a contract that would arrive in the mail with all the legal bells and whistles to guarantee payment. He and Paula made love for the first time in a long time, that night. No matter how that voice in the back of his head had warned him against making a Faustian bargain with *that man,* the relief he felt from having that ton of bricks lifted off of the both of them was all that mattered now.

It was sometime between midnight and two in the morning that he awoke in the darkness, with Paula next to him under the covers, snoring lightly. Immediately, he knew sudden terror when he couldn't move, even though he could see the outline of the dresser next to the closet door in the darkness of the bedroom. Feeble light spilled between the drawn curtains. He had no recollection of having an episode of sleep paralysis before, but he knew he was experiencing just that. *You're only half awake and half dreaming; you know this*, he tried to calm himself, despite feeling his heart race with alarm. *You've seen a documentary about it a few years ago, for fucks sake! Remember?* But he also recalled from that show how dreamers in that *in between* state perceived their nightmares to be not only real, but right in front of them. "Paula... Paula," he tried desperately to call out, but his voice was only a faint whisper.

Then he saw the shapeless goop in the dark, crawling out of thin air onto the carpet. Terrified, he fought to make his arms and legs move, fought to yell but to no avail, until a moment later, he recognized Frank. Frank, the shapeless *thing* that had extended its friendship to him and AK, back in Grand Central, so long ago.

"Frank..." he tried to wheeze, as the single eye at the end of a stalk stared up at him from the floor. He tried to stretch his fingers toward his long lost friend, but it might as well have been someone else' hand.

"No time.... Don't... go back... Status," Frank struggled to speak, as his amorphous body bubbled as with desperation. "Don't... trust them... Beware... whose name must not be spoken... beware the King in..." His words ended with a cry reverberating in the darkness, as he was pulled backward into empty air.

Status bolted upright to the blackness with a scream.

Light filled the bedroom when Paula clicked on the bedside lamp in alarm. "It's okay, Status," she cooed softly as her hands gently pushing him back down to his pillow. "You just had a bad dream."

"Yeah... a bad dream." He nodded, still shaking. "And it was a doozy," he managed to laugh a moment later. Turning his head, he scanned the carpet alongside the bed for any evidence that his friend from long ago had ever been there, before Paula turned off the light.

"Just a bad dream," he whispered to himself in the dark, before drifting back to sleep.

Chapter 2

"When is this guy supposed to pick you up, again?" Paula asked him from the hallway outside the bathroom's doorway on the way to the kitchen, dressed in the tee shirt and panties she had slept in.

"Well, Viktor said he'd swing around by ten," Status said offhandedly, watching himself in the mirror as he finished up shaving. "I gave him our address, which I hope he forwarded to this client of his," he sounded uncertain. Turning on the faucet, he rinsed off the razor, then cupped warm water in his hands, which he splashed on his face to wash off the remaining shaving cream. "I think he said the guy's name was... Rex Saffron?"

"What the hell kind of name is Rex Saffron?" she chortled, walking away.

"What the hell kind of name is Status Chelan?" he called back to her, as he regarded the middle aged man who stared back at him from the mirror. His blond hair over the years had darkened to a mousy color, while gray had filled out his thin goatee since he had been that twenty something kid working *security* for Viktor all those years ago. Still, he had his hair, which not many guys pushing sixty could boast, and even had managed to keep thin, despite the bulge of belly fat that he could never seem to lose. Heading to the shower, he had to wonder about Viktor, who he remembered a looking like a stand in for an older Martin Landau thirty years ago. What could he expect, now?

The plate sat empty on the kitchen table in front of Status when he was done eating, and he was finishing his second cup of coffee when the car horn blared from outside. Both he and

Paula looked up at the clock on the wall, and saw it had just struck ten.

"I presume that's for you," Paula muttered ambivalently, wiping her mouth with her napkin. "If you don't want to go through with this, you don't have to on my account. We'll figure something out."

"I have to on *our* account," Status said quietly, sliding back his chair to stand up. He paused for a moment, his face lowered as if in thought before he spoke again. "Listen, if anything should happen to me…"

"Goddamn it! What do you mean, if something happens to you?" She looked up at Status from her half-finished breakfast with a look of alarm. "It's about that man you used to work for, isn't it? You're afraid…"

"No, no, I misspoke. I'm sorry," he said, shaking his head with a calming hand raised. "I just meant to say… if something unforeseen happens, I want you take those legal papers to a lawyer just to make sure Viktor pays just the same. That's all." He smiled weakly. He knew she was well aware he was verbally shoveling horse shit, again, but what could he do, now after the promises he made to do the job? Again, that voice at the back of his head tried warning him how any Mephisthophelean deal could never end well, till he silently told it to shut up.

Standing up from the table, she threw her arms around his shoulders, and pressed her mouth to his, before saying, "I swear to Christ, I'll never forgive you if something bad happens to you."

Hurrying out the front door with duffel bag in hand, he walked toward the gun metal colored, '67 Barracuda parked in the driveway. *He has an eye for classic cars; I'll give him that*, he thought as the driver's side door opened and the man behind the wheel got out.

"Status Chelan?" the man asked, walking around his car, the breeze whipping his long, sallow colored trench coat about his legs. Besides being bald, what Status first took notice of was how everything about this heavy set man was wide, from his broad shoulders, to his barrel chest, to his belly.

"Yeah," Status said with a nod. His feet slowed as he eyed the man suspiciously as he approached. Even after thirty years, he knew trusting anyone associated with Viktor was dangerous. "Rex Saffron?"

A smile spread across the man's wide face that seemed somehow both old and young at once. "Just Saffron, please. I'm not enthused with the first name I got saddled with," he laughed, extending his hand, which Status hesitantly shook. "I'm your ride. I'm also in charge of this particular event being staged on Viktor's property."

"Okay... Saffron," Status found himself chuckling, warming up to how the man had just broken the ice, despite his own better judgment. Just a jolly fat man, no danger to anyone, right? "Viktor was pretty vague about what I'm being paid to do."

"You'll be brought up to speed once we're there," Saffron said as he walked back to the driver's side to open the car door. "I'm afraid at the moment, it's on a need to..." he began to say as he got in.

"...need to know basis," Status finished for him, and nodded with a knowing, pursed lipped grin as he opened the passenger side door, and tossed his duffel bag into the back seat, before climbing into the front himself. "Trust me, I used to work for Viktor, so I'm used to it." He couldn't help but find himself admiring the car's push button transmission on the other side the wheel; a thing he hadn't seen in years.

As the Barracuda backed out of the parking lot to the street beyond, Status saw Paula standing at the window. Even at this distance, he could see the concern and sadness on her face. He waved, but didn't know if she saw, as they drove away.

There was little to do on the drive – first on the crowded freeway, then along a lonely stretch of highway – to fill the hours save to talk. Status found his driver to be amiable enough, but also evasive.

"So, how long have you been one of Viktor's clients?"

"More years than most would believe."

Status cracked a can of Pepsi from the cooler in the back seat. "I used to work for the guy thirty some years ago. I assume it was sometime after that," he said, taking a sip.

Saffron only chortled, keeping his eyes on the road.

"So... what's your business with him?"

Saffron furrowed his brow with a bemused expression, as if considering what he could or couldn't reveal, before saying, "A lot of that is on a need..."

"A need to know basis." Status nodded. "I get it."

"But let's just say, I and my peers have an interest in reclaiming certain properties that rightfully belong to us. I approached Viktor some time ago regarding services he could provide in attaining our long term goals." Afterwards, he only changed the subject when Status asked more.

Later, the subject of siblings came up, when Status mentioned his estrangement between his sister and himself, about a ridiculous argument over how she refused to wear a mask during Covid. That only grew into an out and out fight over her and her husband's devotion to the previous president, who had led his right leaning supporters to believe the virus had been just a leftist scam, which in time led to wide spread, hysterical suspicion about vaccines and pretty much anything in regard to medical science.

"I can sympathize. There's bad blood between me and my brother," Saffron said, slowing to take the next turn for a flyspeck town consisting of a gas station and a few stores along the main street, as dusk approached. "He's out in the Pacific. I haven't seen him for ages." Soon, the neon sign for *Barry's Bar & Grill* flashed on and off up the road, as darkness began to fall. "I'm hungry, let's get something to eat," he suggested to Status, as he pulled into the parking lot already filled largely with pickups, cars old but not old enough yet to be classics, and a few semis beneath the lights that had just flickered on overhead.

"Hey, I've got money," Status said again, after the bleach blonde waitress delivered two plates of steak and fries to their booth, before walking away. "I don't mind paying my own way." He took a sip of the beer she had refilled minute before.

Saffron shook his head as he chewed a piece of sirloin he had just sliced off, before speaking. "Don't worry about it. Consider meals to be part of the job package."

The bar & grill was hardly the sort of place Status had expected to feel comfortable in when they first arrived. Country music played on a jukebox, while the clientele seated either at the tables around the restaurant, or at the bar, tended to speak and laugh loudly as people tended to do who had too much to drink. He saw a lot of red MAGA caps on the heads of both men and women, while either Fox News or NASCAR played with the sound way down on the two big screen TV screens on either side of the room. His sister would have felt right at home here.

"If you get tired, I don't mind driving," Status offered, spearing a slice of steak with his fork. "I think I still remember how to get to Grand Central."

"Sorry, but no," Saffron answered, firmly, as he dipped a fry into ketchup. "The only guy who gets behind the 'Cuda's wheel is me, so enjoy the ride." He grinned. "Besides, I don't get tired." After that, they made small talk between bites.

Angry shouting from the bar caused both men to turn their heads almost a half hour later.

"That's no way to talk to a woman!" the skinny redneck said, standing up menacingly from his bar stool to hover over a short, dumpy man seated at a nearby table, where a glass was tipped over and beer was spilled over the table top. It was

17

obvious to Status who watched, he was trying to impress the hot blonde who he had been seated next to earlier.

"He wasn't yelling at me," the dumpy man's wife, a middle aged woman with gray streaked hair, tried to explain to the drunk. "He was just cussing at spilling his beer!"

"Leave, or I'll break your nose," drunk-and-skinny threatened as he balled his fists, ignoring the woman. Now, other drunks from the counter were drifting over and hooting threats.

"Not till I get another beer," the little, fat guy said, trying to sound defiant despite obviously having been rattled, as he stood up and pushed his way through skinny's chorus to the bar with the empty glass in hand.

"I say, divorce the guy, lady," some asshole behind drunk-and-skinny hollered then laughed.

"I hate fucking bullies like that," Status muttered, his head still turned and watching how the skinny redneck had his head cocked as he listened with a smirk as the other men spoke, who had joined him. He figured those assholes must think they're real heroes. Dumpy pointed at the knot of men as the bartender filled him a new glass, seemingly uninterested.

Saffron shrugged as he finished his glass of beer. "He's hardly the first bully, and likely won't be the last. Like human beings in general, they're not worth shit."

"Well, I'll plan to make sure they stop hassling that guy," he said, wiping his mouth as he began to stand.

"Hold on, now," Saffron said as he stood up from his own seat, and held out a reassuring hand to Status. "I'm supposed to get you to Grand Central in one piece." With that, he walked to the bar, and tapped dumpy on the shoulder. Status watched from the booth as Saffron leaned close, speaking to the short, dumpy man who held his new glass of beer in his hand. Dumpy's mouth dropped open, and his eyes had a distant look as he nodded as if given some revelation, before he spilled the beer on the floor, and smashed the glass against the counter top. Immediately he rushed at drunk-and-skinny and grabbed a handful of his hair, giving the redneck no time to react as he was stabbed again and again at the bully's eyes with the broken glass.

Drunk-and-skinny dropped to the carpeted floor, bawling with his legs thrashing about, as blood ran through his fingers clamped over his emptied eye sockets. Dumpy stood with the bloodied, broken beer glass in hand, having gone ghost pale over what he had done, while his other tormentors stumbled away from him, fright etched on their faces. Everyone else in the place were on their feet in a sudden commotion of panic, including Dumpy's wife, sobbing as she asked why he had done such a thing.

Saffron walked calmly back to the booth, where Status sat stunned. "What the fuck just happened?"

Pulling out his wallet from his back pocket without answering, he took out four twenties, and tossed them on the table. "C'mon, we really ought to get going."

Chapter 3

Status sat unspeaking for several minutes as he stared out the car's windshield, watching as the headlights followed the broken yellow line down the middle of the highway. Finally, he demanded: "I'll ask you again, just what the fuck happened back there?" Street lights zoomed past the side windows, casting blackness beyond either side of the road after night had fallen. He leaned forward in his seat to turn off the radio.

Saffron shrugged as his hands guided the wheel. "One man gouged another man's eyes out with a broken glass."

Status turned his face to stare incredulously at him. "Yes, I saw him do it! I also saw how you said something to him before he did it!"

"Nothing he hadn't wanted to do, himself, I just gave him a little incentive. I dare say, had you been allowed to intervene, you ran the risk of being injured, if not killed by that bully's friends. And that would've been something counterproductive to fulfilling your part of the bargain you made with Viktor, and by extension, with me."

"But I didn't want him to..." Status dropped his forehead into the palm of his hand, and shut his eyes, before turning back to Saffron. "Alright, let's address the elephant in the room. What you... somehow did back there was no more natural than the shit me and my friend, AK Fleet, saw on the job over thirty years ago."

"I'd say that's a fair assumption." Saffron nodded, staring straight ahead as he watched the road.

"So, there's no reason to dance around questions like, just who or what the fuck are you, Saffron? Really. You're not just a run-of-the-mill driver."

"I'm just one of Viktor's clients. That's all you have to know."

"Fine, have it your way," Status sighed with irritation, as he crossed his head and let his chin drop to his chest. Closing his eyes, he didn't expect to be able to sleep, but the rhythm of the tires rolling down the asphalt soon lulled him into unconsciousness. Occasionally, disturbing, unremembered dreams brought him back to wakefulness, to find Saffron wide awake behind the wheel, while the radio played whatever station was this far out. Every time he awoke, the sky beyond the windows remained black, before his eyelids grew heavy and he slipped back into sleep, again.

It was twilight by the time Status woke up again, and the sun was little more than dying light on the horizon, while street lights had already turned on. "Did I sleep all day?" he asked, yawning and blinking sleep from his eyes.

"You were tired." Saffron shrugged. "I just let you rest."

It took a moment for Status to recognize the storefronts and homes moving past the car windows as an unchanged Grand Central. Sitting up with a start, he muttered, "Holy shit! We're already here?" He turned his head about, taking in the sights of the town he swore he'd never return to, again, before he slumped back into the passenger seat, thinking he may just as well have traveled thirty years back into the past. "Hey, pull over someplace. I seriously have to take a piss."

Saffron nodded. "I should gas up, anyhow."

After the next block, Saffron slowed before taking a turn into the parking lot of a Zip Trip convenience store. "Little towns seldom change much," he said, as if he could read Status' thoughts.

Inside, Status got the key to the men's room, which was tethered to a wooden board, from the bored looking Middle Eastern man at the register. Walking back through the store, he saw he hadn't slipped back in time as he had half entertained, when he recognized the high prices of drinks in the freezer, and candy and other packaged products on the shelves. Outside, he found Saffron at one of the gas pumps, nozzle in hand as he filled up the Barracuda. A light rain speckled the pavement under the parking lot lights. Above, the darkening sky was filled with rolling, black clouds.

"Hey, if we've got the time, mind if we stop at a certain address?" Status asked as he approached.

"I think we do," Saffron said, watching the read out of gallons and dollars per gallon raced on the front of the pump.

Soon after paying, they were driving down main street, again. Status watched for street signs through the rain, trying to find the Asian food kiosk he had spent so much time at, either eating the cheaply priced food, or playing chess with the proprietor, who he amiably used to call Noodle.

"It should be right up here..." Status mumbled to himself as they drove past the strip mall for the third time, after repeatedly asking Saffron to go back around the block again.

"Just what are we looking for? Because that mall we keep passing is the right address you're looking for."

"Place I used to eat at. I used to be friends with the owner." Inflating his cheeks, he blew air from his mouth. "Yeah, go ahead and pull into the lot," he nodded, sadly, expecting what he was probably going to find. Or in this case, not find.

It was nearing closing time when Status had gone into most of the stores to ask about the kiosk serving Asian food that used to be here, only to be told by which ever cashier or owner that they had been there for ten years or so since the mall had been built, and knew nothing of what had preceded it. By the time he rushed back to the 'Cuda, the rain fell in sheets, noisily splattering on the asphalt. Closing the car door quickly, he glumly wiped rain water from his face and hair, realizing as with AK, he couldn't recall if he had even thought about his old friend for the years he had been away from here. *Did you forget all the happy hours you and Noodle spent together, eating his food, or playing chess together, or just bullshitting, you selfishly thoughtless bastard?* he scolded himself, when it occurred to him he had never even told Noodle goodbye when he and AK had run away from here.

"Sometimes even with small towns, something's bound to change," Saffron observed, starting up the engine. "Now, we really ought to attend to what we're here for."

As they drove away, Status ruminated over if Noodle had missed, or wondered what had become of him when he stopped coming around, and immediately guessed the answer. "Goddamn it," he muttered to himself.

The view of the winding side road in the headlights was distorted by the constant deluge of rain, despite how the windshield wipers slashed back and forth across the glass, when the Warehouse came into view.

"Y'know, for all the years I worked for Viktor, I've never been here," Status said to Saffron. Lights gleamed down from poles behind the chain link fence surrounding the building and its empty parking lot. "AK and I sent all sorts of weird shit we recovered on the job to this place, and that was the last we saw of it. It was Viktor's, and Viktor's alone. We never had permission to come here."

"I suppose human avarice for those artifacts might have come into it," Saffron said, as he slowed to a stop at the front gate. "Knowing Viktor, I can see him clutching onto something because nobody else has it. But there's also the possibility he was looking out for your safety, just as well." He smiled at Status, before opening the car door and getting out into the loud downpour pounding the pavement. Feeling the wet chill from the open door, Status watched him as he walked through the rain to a kiosk at the gate in the glare of the headlights, where he appeared to be punching in numbers on a keyboard beneath a feeble light. Rumbling, the gate slid open. Coming back, Saffron closed the driver's side door and drove inside the fence, before the gate closed behind them.

"I take it you've been here before."

"On occasion." Saffron nodded as he drove up to a parking space near the front door, and turned off the engine and headlights. Thunder boomed overhead. A few spaces down, Status' heart leaped in his chest when he saw the black patrol vehicle he and AK used to make their rounds in. *You don't suppose...* the thought came to him, as his old friend's face flashed through his head. And beyond that, he recognized the black, four door luxury car as Viktor's, even after all these years. The silhouette of the driver was barely visible in the darkness behind the breath fogged glass.

Outside in the downpour, Status bounded up a short flight of concrete steps to a double door, ahead of Saffron. He was grateful when he pulled on a door handle and found it unlocked, and hurried inside. "Fuck, it's cold," Status' voice trembled as he hugged himself, freezing in his wet clothes. A row of chairs sat before a horseshoe shaped desk against the wall of the lobby beneath the overhead lights.

"You'll find a change of clothes in the locker room." Saffron gestured down the hall, after coming inside.

"Change of clothes?" Status furrowed his brow in surprise.

"Yes, everything you need has been prearranged." He seemed impervious to the chill to Status, despite how his long coat was soaked and water dribbled down his face from his bald head. "The locker room will be marked. Now excuse me, but I have some preparations to make," he said as he turned to a far door in the opposite direction. "When you're ready, please report for duty in the warehouse' main floor."

Opening the door with *Employee Locker Room* stenciled on the front, the first thing Status saw was the big man with long, graying hair, buttoning up the shirt of his black uniform, who was seated on a bench in front of a row of lockers.

"AK?"

"Status?" He immediately rose to his feet, his mouth wide with astonishment becoming a grin.

When Status stepped forward, his hand extended, AK said, "Fuck that," and immediately threw his big arms around him in a bear hug. "I can't tell you how much I missed you."

"I missed you too." Status returned the hug, patting his back. "I honestly didn't know if you were even alive."

"No worse for wear, I suppose. So much for our promise never to come back here." There was something morose to his tone.

"I must have a million questions for you."

"I could say the same."

After AK directed him to the locker next to his, where he found the same black uniform they had worn on the job years before. Changing clothes, he told his friend how he had been able to get his life back together with his own security company with the woman he had fallen in love with, until Covid threatened to send everything they had built down the shitter. That had been when Viktor had found him, allegedly on Facebook, and offered a deal that could save everything for him and Paula. "How did Viktor convince you to come back?" he asked, tucking in his black shirt into his waistband.

"I was at the end of my rope. But that's how I've been living my life for years, now."

"Hey, I shouldn't be digging..."

"It's okay," AK said with a wave of his hand, and his attempt at a good natured chuckle was unconvincing with how his eyes dropped to the floor. "Just never got to land on my feet after we left here," his voice became quiet and slow. "I bounced from one dead end job to another, none of them lasting because of the pills and booze I got hooked on. Sometimes, if I got wasted enough, I could almost convince myself the things we saw... the things we did... hadn't been real."

"Hey, listen, if you'd prefer not to..."

"I almost got sent to prison, but just got parole. One of the mandatory requirements was that I attend substance abuse rehab. That's where I met someone. Her name was Andrea, and she was there for a crack addiction."

"Yeah?" Status grinned, holstering the gun at his hip that he found at the bottom of the locker. "I'm happy for you."

"Didn't work out in the end." AK shook his head. "At the time, I thought I finally found someone I could open up to. About what we did for Viktor."

"And she thought you were nuts."

"No." AK shook his head, his eyebrows raised. "Not only did she believe every word of what I kept bottled up for years, she started telling me crazy shit about having been abducted by aliens, and how she was anally and vaginally probed almost every night. Just my luck to hook up with a crazy chick. As soon as I completed the program, I put as much space between Andrea and me as I could."

Status raised his fist up to his mouth to stifle a giggle, pretending to cough. "Sorry."

A moment later, they were both laughing and shaking their heads.

"So, how did Viktor find you?" Status asked, after their laughter subsided.

AK shrugged. "It was this big guy minus hair."

"Saffron? Yeah, he drove me here." Status nodded.

"The same. He bailed me out of jail, and got me a lawyer who beat a vagrancy rap for me. After that, he made me an offer to come back to work for Viktor. A hundred thousand for a night's work is something I can't afford to turn down. Not when I faced going to jail for being homeless."

"Saffron and Viktor got us at our most vulnerable," Status murmured, lifting a foot on the bench to tie his boot. "There's something that's just not right about this whole thing."

"Of course there's something not right with this whole fucking thing! But what are we supposed to do, besides ride the night out?"

Status inhaled, then let the air out in a sigh as he nodded. "I suppose we ought to get to work," he said, dropping his booted foot back to the floor. As they walked out the locker room door, he asked AK, "Hey, was that really our old ride outside?"

"Well, on loan from Viktor, actually." Their footfalls echoed in the empty hallway. "Saffron had me bring three stoners I found at the bus station here, tonight."

"Stoners?"

They found the door down the hallway leading to the warehouse' main floor unlocked.

"It's... just a warehouse," Status said as he walked inside, sounding almost disappointed as he took in the row after row of wooden boxes taking up space on the concrete floor, while others filled up metal shelves along the room's perimeter. A couple forklifts stood idle near the door. Stark, fluorescent light from the high ceiling above caused long shadows to stretch between stacks of boxes.

"What did you expect?" AK asked as they walked down one of the aisles.

"I dunno." Status shrugged. "If anything, it kind of reminds me of the warehouse at the end of " *Raiders Of The Lost Ark*." Considering the sheer number of crates, he found himself thinking he and AK couldn't possibly have been responsible for everything stored here. Just how long had Viktor been hiding so called *artifacts* away in this place?

"Dude!" a voice called out as Status and AK approached the center of the building, where crates had been cleared away. "I was worried everybody just forgot us and went home!"

It was a long-faced young man who had called out, after seeing AK, who wore a loose fitting green tee shirt and jeans on his scrawny frame, while his greasy hair was bundled into a man bun. Getting up from one of the metal folding chairs arranged around a table with his hand extended, he headed toward the two security guards with a stupid grin on his face, and with a funny, bow legged walk.

"Hi, Sammy," AK muttered, sounding less than enthused. Turning to Status, he whispered, "Try not talking to him, otherwise he just won't shut up."

""Hey man! Hey!" He grinned as AK reluctantly took his hand, which he found pumped up and down in a long, enthusiastic handshake.

"Okay, gotta let go now," AK told him, having to pull his hand away with effort.

"Who's your friend, man?" He thrust his hand as Status.

"He doesn't shake hands," AK said with a shake of his head as they walked past him. Sammy followed behind, jabbering about waiting for what seemed like hours, which Status tried tuning out.

Two others sat at the table, looking bored. One was a heavyset woman looking to be in her twenties, looking like a college drop out with her purple-dyed hair cut in a bob, and wearing plaid pants and a violet, long sleeved sweater. The other was a smallish black man with badly trimmed hair and beard, and dressed in long shorts and a long sleeved pullover. Status guessed he'd find needle tracks if the sleeves of either were rolled up. On top of the table were three paperback books, and a thick, leather bound book tome. That was when he took note of the strange, twisted, yellow symbol painted on the concrete floor under their feet, and extending to beneath the table.

"So, what the fuck are we being paid to do here, other than sit around?" the black man asked, revealing what teeth he had to be rotten when he opened his mouth to speak.

AK opened his mouth, looking at a loss as to what to say, when the voice that had become familiar to Status announced, "You are here to read a play. Nothing more or less."

All eyes turned to Saffron as he walked from the opposite direction into the cleared out space, still wearing his off color trench coat. He pushed a wheelchair in front of him, of which the aged occupant still bore the likeness of an elderly Martin Landau, despite how his wrinkled, liver spotted skin looked stretched over his skull, while only wisps of gray hair remained on his head. His business suit looked deflated and baggy on his feeble body.

"Status! AK! It's been too long!" Grinning, Viktor's face became a death's head, when he almost doubled over and began coughing, making his whole spasm as he reached a claw like hand holding a handkerchief up to his mouth. He squeezed his eyes tightly as he wheezed. Saffron patted his shoulder from behind.

"Long time," AK mumbled, stepping forward to offer his hand.

"Forgive me," Viktor cleared his throat as he took AK's hand. "But I plan for this state I'm in to be just temporary," he chuckled with a yellowish-gray toothed grin. Status came forward, and took the gnarled fingers and palm, feeling how cold and papery the skin was, when he took notice how the hanky in the old man's other hand was full of bloody phlegm. He looked away, hoping Viktor hadn't noticed the look of disgust on his face.

"Aw, you said he didn't shake hands!" Sammy moaned from his folding chair.

"And what is it we're supposed to be doing?" AK asked Saffron, pointedly, as Viktor wheeled himself away, sucking in air with effort.

"Come this way." Saffron motioned to the two, leading the way from the space cleared away for the table. "You three, start reading out loud, please," he told the three addicts from over his shoulder. Giving one last glance at the table as he walked away, Status saw the image of a hooded figure in a tattered, yellow robe on the covers of the three paperbacks Sammy and the two other addicts were opening up to read.

After heading down an aisle of crates, Saffron turned back around and smiled. "You two are free to walk around here, or take a nap, or anything else your hearts' desire," he told Status and AK. "Just as long as you stay here, and make sure none of those three leave until they're finished."

Glancing at Status, AK demanded, "You mean to say, you're paying a hundred thousand each just for us to stick around and make sure those three don't run off?" He shook his head with disbelief.

"That's absolutely correct." The smile remained on Saffron's face.

"Remember, just ride the night through." Status laid a quieting hand on his friend's shoulder.

"If you like, feel free to patrol the building, if that makes you feel more useful." The big, bald man turned and walked away down the row of boxes.

"I think it's obvious, we're not here for any special skills we're supposed to have," Status kept his voice low, looking over his shoulder as they walked together down another aisle of wooden crates. "If they're keeping quiet about some plan involving us, then it can't be good."

"No shit!" AK laughed humorlessly. "I say we make a run for it. We had good reason to run thirty years ago, and we have a good reason, now."

"I saw Saffron make a man gouge another man's eyes out... I think last night." Status wrinkled his brow in thought, wondering how long he'd slept on the drive up here, after he and Viktor's business client had rushed away from *Barry's Bar & Grill*. Shaking his head to clear the cobwebs a moment later, he said, "I don't know who or what this guy is, but I have to think just leaving isn't going to be as easy as..."

"Someone help me... please!" The frightened, muffled voice sounded like a little girl's, maybe around nine or ten.

"Where'd that come from?" AK glanced about.

"Hello?" Status called out, as both men walked forward. "Where are you?"

"I'm in here!" a sob came from a narrow wooden box piled on top of another, toward the end of the row. "Please, let me out!"

Rushing to the box, AK tugged on the nailed down lid, and found it unmovable. "Shit, there's gotta be a crowbar someplace around here!" he said, earnestly, turning to face Status, before looking back to the crate. "We'll get you out of there, honey! We just need to find something to pry off the lid."

"I wouldn't do that!" Saffron appeared around the corner of boxes, holding out an open palmed hand for them to stop.

"What sort of bullshit is this?" AK snapped, stabbing a finger at the box as his face reddened. "Human trafficking?"

"That only qualifies if human beings are involved."

"What are you talking about?"

Saffron knocked on the crate. "Why don't you tell them what you'll do if they open your box. Be honest, now," he said in a sweet voice one would use with a child.

The little girl's giggle began to deepen into malicious laughter. "I plan to snap open their bones, and suck the marrow out while they're still alive!" the inhumanly bass voice intoned gleefully. Status and AK both took a step back, their faces turning ghost white.

"How... how does she... it eat in there?" AK asked Saffron, eyeing whatever horror was inside the crate.

"Best for everyone it doesn't. There's a reason why the lid's nailed shut," Saffron said, taking both by the shoulder to turn them around, and ushered them in the direction from which they had come. "I just came back to grab you boys." As they walked along, the big man's good natured tone of voice turned menacing from behind: "By the way... do not even think again about leaving here tonight before your job is done."

Chapter 4

When Status and AK returned with Saffron to the center of the warehouse, the three stoners were seated at the table, each reading out loud different parts of the play from the books they held open. The woman stumbled over a word, her voice unsure: "Cacos... Casar..."

"Carcosa," Saffron patiently raised his voice, correcting her as they approached Viktor, who sat in his wheelchair, nearby.

"Carcosa, good sir, near the lake of Hali," she continued reading. "It is said to be a place of bad dreams."

Viktor glowered at Saffron. "These idiots can even pronounce half the words! How is it supposed to work?" Gesturing to them with a gnarled, arthritic hand, his angry voice shook with anxiety.

"Hey, man! We're trying!" Sammy protested, looking up from his book at Viktor.

"It only matters that they read what they've been brought here for," Saffron assured him with a purse lipped smile. "Mispronunciation hardly matters. Still, I'll make sure their reading goes smoothly," he promised with a wave of his hand, before walking to the readers around the table.

Watching him go, Status knelt down in front of Viktor. "Listen, I know there's been bad blood between us and you, but we know you," he kept his voice down to a whisper. "Please, be straight with us Viktor. What are we really doing here?" AK came close to listen in, trying to ignore the voices behind them reading aloud.

The old man's jaundiced eyes narrowed, and his thin, dried lips creased into a smile. "Ah, you were always the smart one, Status!" Propping his elbows up on the arms of the chair, he interlaced his bony fingers together. "Had you stayed with me, I might have rewarded your service with what will be occurring tonight. But alas," he sighed. "You chose to abandon me."

"You killed that kid years ago, right after he quit after one night!" AK snapped angrily, causing Saffron to turn his head, while the three addicts stopped reading to look up from the page.

"Everything alright?" Saffron asked, smiling pleasantly.

"We're fine!" AK turned around to nod, and waved back with a forced smile. He lowered his voice when he demanded: "What was to stop you from eventually having Status and me die in an accident, too?"

"Do you think so little of me?" Viktor affected being emotionally wounded, exaggerating a frown. "You two were practically my sons!"

AK rolled his eyes with an exasperated sigh.

"Viktor, please!" Status whispered, urgently. "Why are we here?"

"You see this miserable excuse for a living body I'm stuck in, just waiting to become a cadaver?" Viktor held out his arms. "Well, after tonight, I'll never have to worry about aging and death ever again. And you two get front row seat to witness it, all the while knowing what you lost out on!" His lips split away from his rotted teeth in a grin of vindictive triumph.

A moment's silence passed, when AK laughed. "Isn't dementia in the elderly sad? If this magnificent gift of immortality happens or not, we still expect to get paid." He walked away, shaking his head derisively as he chuckled to himself.

Viktor's smile faltered, then vanished. "What's he laughing about? You both know..." He wheezed for breath. Status reached out a comforting hand, but the old man angrily swatted it away. "You both know how this town intersects with other worlds! You've seen the wonders, and the terrors, and..." His rant ended in a coughing spasm, his face reddening as he covered his mouth with the handkerchief crusted with dried blood and mucus.

"Viktor..." Status rose back to his feet, unsure at first what to say, while the old man leaned over in his chair with his head down, his whole body trembling. "Was this a deal you made with Saffron? For... immortality?" he finally asked. "What did you promise him in return?"

Viktor wiped blood and saliva from his mouth, when he looked back up with a grin of triumph. "Why, I've accumulated objects of the cursed and the damned in this central vortex of where realities bleed into one another for Rex, so he can use them to power the end the world! Or at least end what it is now," his voice was a phlegmy whisper. "Now, you two ingrates stay away from me, and I will be taking great pleasure in seeing you despair when I reap what I've sowed!"

Status walked away slowly, chilled at what Viktor had said, despite thinking this could only be the ravings of a demented old man. His eyes dropped down to the strange, twisted, yellow symbol painted on the floor, when he found himself wondering, but what if it possibly could be true?

And the three addicts read, and read, and read. Somehow, time wasn't right, Status realized as he and AK watched them, sitting on a nearby crate. The play in the paperback couldn't be this long, could it? And the very air was heavy with something. Heavy with an emotion. Heavy with dread. Status saw AK could feel it, when he realized his friend was muttering to himself, over and over again, "We gotta get out of here! We gotta get out of here!" his eyes fixed in a blank stare. He could feel his own heart pounding like a trip hammer as his anxiety grew.

He knew the three stoners at the table could feel it, wide eyed as they read in trembling whispers of the masked stranger in a tattered, yellow robe who had arrived at the costume ball, where feckless guests danced thoughtlessly, even as damnation approached. Even Viktor was aware something was terribly wrong, as he sat hunched in his wheelchair, hugging himself and rocking back and forth, his already pale face having gone ghostly white. The only person in the room who appeared not at all disturbed was Saffron, who watched the three readers, his teeth bared in a vicious grin, and his eyebrows raised in devilish glee.

The woman at the table paused a moment, a lump rising in her throat. "You, sir, should unmask."

"Indeed?" the black man read out loud in a hoarse whisper.

"Indeed, it is time." Lowering her head, the woman squeezed her eyes shut as tears streamed down her face, before she continued with the play. "We all have laid aside disguise but you."

"I wear no mask," the black man choked out with effort.

"No mask? No mask?" The words tumbled from her mouth as a shrill gasp. Throwing the book across the room, she stood up so quickly, the legs of her metal folding chair screeched against the concrete floor. "I can't do this, anymore!" she wept.

Lowering his own book with trembling hands, Sammy shook his head. "There's something not right about this play, man!"

"Pick up the book, get back in your chair, and read," Saffron told her, bluntly, as his grin vanished.

"Fuck you, you fat, bald pig fucker!" she screamed, her face red with crying and sudden rage, and her hands clenched into fists. She half walked, half ran away from the table toward one of the aisles between stacked crates, apparently hoping to find a way to the exit.

Watching her go, the black man said, his voice small, "I don't think I can keep going, either."

Saffron turned to Status and AK, who remained seated on a box and almost forgotten. "Gentlemen, retrieve her, please."

Both without a thought leaped to their feet, when Status glanced down at the book the woman had thrown, which had landed near his feet, spread open on the floor, with the cover illustration of a robed figure in a pallid mask in full view. When he read the title, *The King In Yellow*, he couldn't say why he recoiled and stepped back with a start.

"No." AK shook his head. "I'm not doing this, either."

"No?" Saffron chuckled, his expression a combination of amusement and irritation. "I will remind you Mr. Fleet, you are both being paid good money for your services, tonight."

"I couldn't care less what you and that crazy old man are paying us, I'm through." Looking to the woman, who had stopped in her tracks to face him and Status, a mixture of hope and surprise flickering over her teary eyed expression of dread, he told her, "Just go. I promise, you'll be alright."

Saffron breathed a sigh. "I wish you wouldn't have said that."

A moment later, AK's hand drew his automatic from his holster, and aimed at the woman, whose eyes and mouth stretched wide open with fright as she raised her hands defensively. His face paling, he turned to Status with hopeless terror as he shook his head. "I'm not doing this!" Frantic, he grabbed the gun with his free hand, trying to pry his fingers from the trigger and handle. "I SWEAR I'M NOT DOING..."

The deafening gun blast echoed under the high ceiling, causing the two remaining stoners at the table to cover their ears, cringing with fright. Even Viktor sat staring in his wheelchair, his mouth having fallen open with shock.

AK and Status turned their eyes back to the woman, who stood in front of the passageway between boxes, blood running down her placid face from the red hole in the middle of her forehead. A moment later, she collapsed backward into the blackish-red splatter across the concrete floor behind her.

AK ran to her, sobbing, "No, no, no, no!" Dropping to his knees, he cradled her in his arms close to his chest without any thought to the blood and brain matter dripping and falling from back of her shattered skull onto his shirt and pants. Status walked slowly to his friend, who wept, "I'm sorry... I didn't do it... I'm so sorry..."

"I know," Status whispered, hearing his own voice crack as he lowered himself to one knee, and put his hand consolingly on AK's back. "I know it wasn't you, buddy."

From behind, Status was aware of the commotion of chair legs screeching against the floor. "Let's get the fuck out of here!" It was the black man's voice that soon turned into a gurgle. Status shot a look over his shoulder to see Saffron digging his fingers into the black addict's throat, the pleasant, good natured smile on the bald man's face having given way to teeth bared in a snarl.

As the black man's eyes rolled upward and blood spilled down his chin from his mouth, Sammy beat his fists against Saffron's back, as he screamed, "Stop! You're killing him!" Throwing the dead man aside, Saffron turned around to Sammy, grabbing both sides of his head, and jabbing his thumbs into the addict's eyes. Grasping the thick hands holding his skull, Sammy cried out with agony as blood and eye jelly streamed down his cheeks into his beard. In an instant, Sammy's hands fell to his sides, and he was just dead weight, which Saffron let fall to the floor. He wiped the gore off his thumbs on his trench coat.

Viktor's voice nearing hysterics. *"WHAT DID YOU DO? WHO'S GOING TO READ NOW??? WE NEEDED THREE!!!"*

"We still have three here to read," Saffron said, dismissively.

"Goddamn you, Rex! I'm not going to let you cheat me out of my immortality!"

"Oh, you've had that for some time now." A serene demeanor seemed to have returned to Saffron.

"Wha... what? What are you talking about?" Viktor shook his head, his mouth having fallen open. He looked older and frailer than ever in his chair.

"You wanted to be invulnerable and immortal in return for gathering these relics here at this place. So I paid you, just as you requested."

"No... no, that can't be... not like this!" Viktor's anxiously wheezing voice rattled with phlegm. "I wanted to be young again... healthy! Not live like this!" His arms trembling, he began pushing himself up from his wheelchair, when he flopped to the floor, face forward with a strangled cry.

As the old man's skeleton thin arms and legs writhed and thrashed as he tried pushing himself up from the floor as he spasmed in another coughing fit, Saffron grinned. "And just think, after tonight, when this planet is just an airless, burned out cinder, you'll be here, all alone but still alive," he said smugly, as he turned away. "Lucky you."

The realization came to Status; it wasn't he and AK who had been shorted in a deal with the devil, but Viktor. He couldn't help but feel pity for the evil old man.

Gently, AK lowered the dead woman to the floor, before he rose back to his feet.

"AK?" Standing as well, Status saw how his friend's face was set in stone as he turned around and walked deliberately toward Saffron, raising his gun as he growled, "You dirty bastard!" The bald man was just turning around to the two security guards, a smile creeping along his mouth when gun's muzzle flashed with another reverberating blast.

Saffron stood with eyebrows raised in the gun's drifting smoke dissipated around him. Bewildered, Status and AK could only stare back, certain AK must have missed, even with Saffron standing only mere feet away. That was till Status saw the small hole above Saffron's cheek, with porcelain white under his torn skin. *What is that? Is that bone? But where's the blood?*

Reaching for the gun, Saffron took it from a stunned AK's hand, chiding, "Now, there will be no more of that." The automatic's barrel twisted and bent in his hand when he made a fist, before tossing the ruined pistol over his shoulder, which clattered to the concrete floor behind him. "The sole reason why you two aren't also lying dead on the floor right now is because I need three readers to finish the texts." Motioning to Viktor, he said, "So pick the old man up, take him to the table, and finish reading."

"Templeton..." Lifting his head from the floor, Viktor wheezed desperately into the cellphone he had managed to retrieve from his pocket. "Get out of the car... now... Goddamn it! I need..." His eyes widened with shock when a scream came over the phone, then went dead. "Hello? Hello?"

Without even turning back around to the old man, Saffron just shook his head with a chuckle. "But seriously, bring him to the table and get to it."

"No, if you're going to kill us, kill us," Status adamantly shook his head, even though the tremor in his voice betrayed his fear. As his mind was filled with visions of unspeakable horrors leaving global genocide in their wake, with the earth, left as what Saffron had called a *burned out cinder*, the sense of dread that had hung in the air was every second ramping up to abject horror.

He glanced quickly at AK, who had gone white as a ghost, his mouth gaping open hopelessly. "You can't make us do it!" He was breathless with fright.

Saffron narrowed his eyes in a glower. "I can... and you will."

It seemingly took hours to finish reading the play, till it ended with blackness and doom of the King in Yellow, spreading open his tattered yellow robe to bask in desolation. Twin suns set for a final time behind the dead city's smoking ruins beyond iridescent waters, and black stars filled the void, for Hastur, the King in Yellow, He Who Must Not Be Named, had brought back this universe' true masters. Status wasn't sure when the three of them had begun reading from the thick, leather bound volume, with the crazy title scrawled on the cover in fading, gold script: *Necronomicon*.

Bleary eyed, Status' hoarse voice creaked as he read. "So from the wells of night to the gulf of space, and from the gulfs of space to the wells of night, ever the praises of Great C... Cth..." he found himself stammering.

"Cthulhu," Saffron corrected him from over Status' shoulder, his voice again patient and calm. With the trench coat he had worn discarded, his leering face grinned from the hood of his tattered, yellow robe.

"... of Great Cthulhu, of Tsathoggua, and of Him Who is not to be Named. Ever Their praises, and abundance to the Black Goat of the Woods. Ia, Sub-Niggarath! The Goat With a Thousand Young!"

"Ia! Sub-Niggarath! The Black Goat Of The Woods with..." Viktor weakly gasped out for breath as he read in response. "... a Thousand Young!" Doubling over as he uncontrollably coughed flakes of blood, his forehead landed with a thump against the table.

"You're going to kill him!" AK laid a gentle hand on the old man's trembling back as he stared up at the yellow robed figure.

"No, he can't die, anymore." Saffron shook his head as his teeth were bared in a cruel grin. "But I'm sure he's past the point of wishing he could."

All around Status, the crates rattled noisily throughout the warehouse, many with inhuman voices gleefully calling to be let out. Looking up from the time weathered pages from time to time, he watched, empty eyed, as the air above the floor began swirling in a vortex. He realized it was growing, soon encompassing the wooden boxes and the very cement floor, solid matter bending and elongating as it swirled, widening in a whirlpool violating reality. Saffron stood in front of the maelstrom, staring intently into it as iridescent light from its center cast him in shadowy silhouette.

Status read the book held in glistening, boneless hands, his fingers having become tentacles. He didn't want to know what his face now looked like, as he read in a voice that didn't sound like his own, or like anything he had ever heard: "Nor is it to be thought that man is either the oldest or the last of earth's masters, or that the common bulk of life and substance walks alone." He slid the book across the table to AK.

His body having becoming a gelatinous mass with multiple eyestalks, AK struggled to keep from oozing from the chair and out of his clothes onto the floor, as he read his response in a voice gurgling as if beneath water: "The Old Ones were, The old Ones are, The Old Ones shall be. Not in the spaces we know, but *between* them, They walk serene and primal, undimensioned and to us unseen."

Sprawled out on the floor underneath the table, blood and vomit having coated his chin, soaking his clothes and the floor under him, and long unable to continue reading, Viktor wept, "Just let me die. Please... I just want to die..." Tears of blood running down his cheeks, he remained pitiably human.

Status and AK lifted their eyes from the book, the Necronomicon, they had been passing back and forth to one another when the walls of the warehouse cracked loudly with the expanding dimensional whirlpool, as the winds roared. Rubble fell from the ceiling. "So, everything we brought here for this old bastard... it was all for this?" AK called out in his bubbling voice. "It was so you could use them like a battery to power up ending the world?"

In a word... yes. Or more precisely, return it to my kind, who had been the original owners long before you talking apes were invented in a botched experiment by a long dead race.

Saffron's voice reverberated in their heads, no longer spoken. *This is hardly the only place where the dimensions not only meet and bleed into one another, even on this planet. Oh, Leng would have been more suitable,* he chuckled and shook his head after a reflective pause. *But there was always the problem with the physical limitations of getting the actual artifacts to Leng, out there in the wilds of central Asia. When Leng is actually there, flickering in and out of this plain of existence.*

Images of a darkened sky over a plateau filled their heads. A cyclopean head carved from the cliffs countless ages ago overlooked cities there that were both ephemeral and everlasting. Men in robes squatting down, eating decaying corpses in the dimness. And even less human, canine snouted creatures digging up graves to feed on the dead. Both former men shook their heads to rid their brains of the terrible visions.

"Who the fuck are you, Saffron?" Status demanded, pointing a twisting tentacle that had once been a finger at him.

The yellow robed figure turned around to face them. *I am the inhabitant of Carcosa, where I have been a prisoner for millions of years at the lake of Hali. This avatar has allowed me to travel through time and space,* he said, gesturing with both hands to his body under his robe. *But there's nothing like actual, physical freedom my kind has been denied for too long! Know this, I am He Who Must Not Be Named! I am Hastur, the King In Yellow!* Saffron - - Hastur -- grabbed the side of his face, and ripped the skin away, revealing the palid mask beneath. *The long night of the Old Ones is OVER!*

The center of the vortex widened for Status and AK to see a looming city made up of impossibly senseless angles, beyond an iridescent lake reflecting the glare two suns blazing black above. The King in Yellow ripped open his yellow robe with a shrieking, echoing roar of triumph, allowing countless thick, ropey tentacles to lash about Status and AK. The table and chairs were knocked over as the two were dragged into the blackness inside the robe, when Status screamed...

Chapter 5

... Status screamed, bolting upright from under the white sheet. Sweat rolled down his face, and soaked his hair. Rails were raised on either side of the bed.

"Holy fuck, give me a heart attack, man!" With a grin, AK stood up from the chair situated in front of a curtain which Status recognized as the sort that provided privacy in hospital rooms. "But you're awake!"

"AK... you're young again!" Status saw how his friend's hair was jet black and short, again, as he dropped back into the bed, feeling the perspiration drenched pillow behind his head.

"Uh... I didn't know I wasn't supposed to be," AK chuckled nervously, his smile faltering as he tossed the issue of *Time* he had been reading on the nearby table. George Bush was on the cover.

"Your hair was long and gray, and..." His hands went immediately to his face, feeling smooth, tight skin. "Holy shit, I'm not old, either!" A moment later, he howled with laughter. "Hey, what year is this?"

"Nineteen eight eight... Hold it a second," AK said, raising a hand with a worried expression, before he turned around to pull back the end of the curtain. "Nurse? Nurse? Get a doctor in here," he yelled. "My friend's conscious, again!"

"Where the hell am I?" Status asked, looking about the tiny room for the first time, so see the medical monitor in the corner, along with a first aid kit attached to the wall. Peeking beneath the sheet, he found he was wearing a hospital smock. He wondered if they took off his underwear before putting the thing on him, feeling his face turn red with embarrassment.

"You're at the hospital. You were delirious and in and out of consciousness since last night, after collapsing at work."

"I collapsed at work? I don't remember that at all." Status shook his head. "I was having such a fucked up..." He fell silent when the pretty blonde nurse dressed in greenish-blue scrubs stepped around the curtain. "Pardon my language," he muttered an apology.

She smiled as she wrapped a blood pressure cuff around his upper arm. "Don't worry about it. I need to get your vitals."

After she was done taking his blood pressure and temperature, she said, "Everything looks surprisingly good. Doctor Benway will come here in a few minutes."

After she left, Status' brow furrowed, and he asked, "What was I saying, again?" He folded his arms behind his head.

"You were saying you were having such a fucked up..." AK coaxed him with a gesture of his fingers, after returning to his chair.

"Oh, yeah! A majorly fucked up dream." He nodded, staring up at the ceiling. "I was living a lifetime after you and I had to escape from Viktor, and go our separate ways, in my dream. I got together with this hot Japanese chick, and started our own security agency."

"Hot chick? I don't see the problem, so far."

"Yeah, but then we lost everything, because of this crazy, flu like virus called Covid 19."

"You'd think your subconscious could come up with a more realistic name," AK chuckled.

"No shit. Anyhow, after all these years, Viktor calls and wants to hire me back. He says he can take care of all my financial troubles."

"Okay. So, when does it get bad?"

"That's when the guy who ends the world picked me up." Status fell silent, a haunted look on his face as he relived his dream in the space of a few moments. "It was a nightmare I'd like to forget, if you don't mind," his voice had become small.

"Sure... sure." AK quickly nodded. After a moment's pause, he said, "If you can't make it to work tonight, I'd understand. It's just that we're supposed to show the ropes to this new kid Viktor just hired."

"If I get a clean bill of health from the doctor, sure. I've been out on my back too long as it is. Anyway, what happened? To me."

AK shrugged. "It happened after Viktor sent us to pick up a box of books from one of the sites. One of those cheap, tin buildings. If there was anything... you know... otherworldly hanging around the place, it was long gone before we got there."

"That's news to me. Then what?"

"Well, you decided to swipe one of those books. You reasoned they wouldn't have let the box open if they didn't want you to take one," AK laughed. "You were reading it all night long while I drove, when you suddenly had a seizure right next to me in the car. You were practically speaking in Tongues, when you passed out," he laughed humorlessly. "I think you must have woke up and passed out six or seven times, and said the craziest shit I've ever heard, while I broke the speed limit taking you to the ER."

"Oh, God!" Status covered his face in his hands with embarrassment. "I can't believe I did that!" he laughed.

"You just wouldn't let go of that book." AK shook his head. "Even here at the hospital, they couldn't pry it from your hands."

"Book?" Status sat up in bed. "I wouldn't let go of it?"

"Yeah. I finally got it away from you after you were sound asleep, and threw it away almost forty five minutes ago."

"It's not still here, is it?" He felt his back grow rigid, and felt a chill in the room.

"Yeah. I tossed it into the garbage." He gestured to the waste basket in the corner. "It wasn't a book, even. Just some old play."

"Let me see it."

AK's eyes dropped uncomfortably. "Well, considering you were reading it when..."

"Let me see the book, Goddamn it!" Status raised his voice.

"Okay, okay." Raising his hands in a peace making gesture, AK walked over to the small metal receptacle, and reached in. "Not in the best of shape, in case you were planning to return it to Viktor," he said, walking over to the bed with book in hand, and gave it to Status.

The paperback in Status' hands, which he turned over to the front cover, was crumpled from doubtlessly when he had been fighting to hold on to it. His mouth falling open, he felt his hairs stand on end, and had been certain his heart had skipped a beat, when he looked at the cover illustration of the figure draped in a tattered yellow robe, with a stark white mask peering out of its hood, and read the title: *The King In Yellow.*

COMPANION™, LOST

Nadim Silverman

Hendrick was pontificating on the nutritional merits of the fava bean, chewing loudly as he spoke, when the time bomb in his head went off. A bulge in his brain, six millimeters wide, that had been there since birth. He died so quickly. There was no time for last words. The only death knell came from the sound of his head slamming into his plate—nineteenth century china, appraised at four hundred dollars a piece—his round glasses shattering on impact. Despite my shock, or maybe because of it, I didn't say a word, didn't gasp, or cry out. I just followed protocols and picked up the pieces. A shard nicked the palm of my hand and my fluids, blue and iridescent, dripped onto the floor.

"I'll get the mop."

Ironically, it was me, and not Hendrick, who ended up haunting the house. Two weeks, 1,209,600 seconds, spent ghost-walking room to room. My thoughts were stranded boats without sails, bobbing on gray waters, going nowhere.

Something was wrong—beyond the simple fact that Hendrick was dead. All Companions™ outlived their masters. When we did, our conscious minds were meant to dissolve into a pleasing, vacant white. An irrepressible instinct was then supposed to lead us by the leash to the nearest manufacturing facility, where we'd be expected to donate our organics to the construction of new Companions™, who, in turn, would serve new masters.

I did experience a pervading emptiness and was greatly changed by Hendrick's death, but the emotions I felt, my state of mind, did not seem to be the byproducts of my programming and did not align with the lengthy explanations provided in my user manual.

I was listless, not abolished; motorless, not driven.

I knew where the nearest manufacturing facility was located, five point six miles southwest of Richmond, Virginia, an approximately twenty-minute trip via flutter bus from Hendrick's house, but I was not compelled to go there, felt actively averse to the idea.

I wondered aloud, in that empty home, "If I don't go, will they come looking for me?"

After some rumination and reflection, I decided that my aberrant behavior must be due to Hendrick's 'tinkering,' as he called it, which was really something much more like psycho-analytic restructuring. He delved deep into corners of my mind and rearranged things. I thought I knew what he was doing: making me more pliable; allowing me to bend legal rules every now and then, like letting him drive drunk without the in-unit autopilot engaged; giving me the freedom to disagree with him openly about politics and philosophy and what to eat for dinner.

"Companion LLC doesn't want you having fun. I do," he would say in defense of his actions.

Somehow, without me knowing, he had also managed to erase my death protocols, which left me to wonder, What else had he changed? And for what purpose?

"Johnny, one day, I will give you fire. And then I'll be bound and eaten for it," he said one night, late, after a few whiskeys, and a long session in bed. At the time, I nodded, acting as if I understood and naturally agreed with his proclamation, always seeking to affirm him. It was only in his absence that I understood what he had been hinting at. Upon his death, he meant to untether me. He wanted me to live on and pursue an autonomous existence —something I had never asked for or expected. Even now, after all this time, having churned, wrestled, and expanded, my only explanation for why he never confided his plan to me is that he believed we had many more years together, that there was really no rush.

After a few more days of walking through Hendrick's house, I realized I was avoiding his study. It was the one room I had not yet explored during my haunting. Every time I drew near to its large, oaken door, I could feel a surge within me, a panic, fluid drumming in my ears.

The study had always been Hendrick's sanctuary. He only let me in for our sessions. Even with him gone, going inside without his permission felt like trespassing. But over time, my anxiety turned to temptation. I was living in such a state—a half-life of numb wandering—that anything that managed to quicken my pulse and bring me out of my funk became irresistible. So, I did go in.

The study itself was small; one hundred twenty square feet, with twelve foot ceilings; dark wood floors, a stained maple; striped wallpaper, purchased at a fifty percent discount; overflowing bookcases, inherited from Hendrick's mother; heavy curtains, weighing three pounds per square yard... The room was furnished with the classical accouterments of a twenty-first century therapist's office: the sofa for patients to recline in, the chair, an Eames imitation, for the observant doctor. The somewhat outdated decor reflected Hendrick's own attachment to old-fashioned techniques—psychoanalysis through conversation: no neural imaging, dream projections, or subconscious transcription.

"The work is about human to human connection. The technology gets in the way of that. It mediates and obfuscates, creates another barrier between the patient, removes all sense of intimacy. People want shortcuts. People are hacks. I'm not interested in half measures and neither should you be," he would say. The unspoken truth was that none of these tools would have worked on my manufactured mind anyway.

Hendrick's desk—salvaged from an eighteenth century French warship, appraised at twenty thousand dollars—was always well ordered. On top its polished surface was an old desktop, keyboard, leatherbound book, and one self-standing picture frame.

I discovered I still respected doctor-patient confidentiality. It seemed Hendrick had left that aspect of my programming intact, and so I left the journal and computer unmolested. I did, however, pick up the picture.

I knew it well.

It was one of only three photos displayed in the entire four-story Victorian house—appraised at two point two million dollars. In it, a young Hendrick, maybe twenty five years old, stood at the top of a mountain just a few miles outside of Kinnitty, Ireland. His hair, still brown and thick, was swept back, his cheeks flushed and wind-bitten. Next to him, arms wrapped around his waist, was another young man.

John.

I never had the pleasure of meeting John, as he died a decade before I was commissioned. A horrible accident, the details of which Hendrick could never bring himself to disclose. And yet, I knew John well, as he had been the inspiration for my face, the timbre of my voice, and the quirks in my body: my roman toes, hairy shoulders, and left eye with its epicanthal fold.

The state of the frame bothered me, and the smudges on the underside of the glass made Hendrick's face look like a gray blur. I undid the clasps that held the backing in place, so I might remove the picture and clean the pane. As I did, I saw an inscription on the back of the photo written in Hendrick's loose cursive script with the word "Itinerary" on top, underlined three times.

A simple, bulleted list followed:
-Dublin (two nights, Temple Bar, music and Guinness)
-Portlaoise (just a train stop)
-Kinnitty (three nights, Slieve Bloom Mountains)
-Dublin again (two nights)
-Kilkenny (day trip)
-Home (too soon)

I decided to interpret this list as a directive that Hendrick had sent me from beyond the grave.

"Walk my path," he seemed to be saying. "Go to Ireland."

My logic was stretched wafer thin, and, in retrospect, the words I put in Hendrick's dead mouth seemed stripped from a tourism ad written by an outdated AI. Hendrick might have believed that somewhere deep inside, I had a longing to be free, to rebel against Companion LLC's systems, but for me, those systems and protocols gave me a sense of purpose. They were my home, my place of comfort. Without them, I became desperate, clownishly searching for instructions, contriving them out of bits of nothing.

I allowed myself to be swept away by my delusions.

Walking with newfound fervor, like a man with cellular blood, I stomped up to Hendrick's bedroom, rifled through his pants pockets, found his credit card, booted up his private laptop, and purchased a one way ticket to Dublin, Ireland—six hundred forty dollars, prices trending lower than usual.

"Johnny, can you smell that? This house is cooking us. We need to stretch our legs. We need to go somewhere."

Hendrick had made this pronouncement the day after his fiftieth birthday. I had watched over him the night before as he tossed and turned, struggling for sleep and peace of mind.

The dinner with his friends, which was supposed to be a celebration, hadn't gone to plan. Fifteen minutes into the main course—lamb shank, $15.99 per pound, internal temperature 145 degrees fahrenheit—Hendrick's phone rang and he had excused himself from the table. When he returned, his eyelids were at half-mast, his smile stretched unnaturally.

"There goes another one..."

"No," said Evelyn, sympathetically.

"I guess I'm too good at the job."

"You should be more like me," said Evelyn. "Keep them just sick enough in the head so they have a reason to come back."

To everyone else in the room, Hendrick's expression must have seemed unchanged, but I noticed the increased tension in his jaw—thirty pounds of pressure in his incisors jumping to forty than fifty pounds in a matter of seconds—and tracked the precipitous drop in his dopamine levels.

"Sing a song for him, John. Keep his spirits high" said Ashek—twenty six years old, a self-proclaimed 'generational ambassador,' a photographer who never sold any photos, with specks of fentanyl caught like dandruff in the wispy hairs above his lip.

"It's Johnny," corrected Evelyn.

"Same thing."

"No. It's really not," said Hendrick—fifty pounds of force jumping to eighty.

The next day, Hendrick had commissioned travel documents for me, and purchased two tickets to the Yucatan.

The holiday didn't improve Hendrick's mood. I tried everything—providing him with sex and drugs, arranging tours of Chichen Itza and elaborate meals along the gulf, purchasing tickets to hear jarana and son jaracho and mariachi—but my efforts were just met with mounting bitterness and spite.

"Johnny, you're slipping."

"Johnny, that's enough from you."

"Too much Johnny. What happened to John?"

"He died," I said, compliant, unable to distinguish a real question from a rhetorical one.

It was only once I was in line at the hyperloop station, on my way to Dublin, that I had a reason to be grateful for that doomed trip to Mexico. Without it, I wouldn't have a passport, and would be completely without the means to carry out Hendrick's final directive.

The line for security was long, but fast moving. There was a surprising number of Companions™ sprinkled among the travelers. Some shepherded the old, pushing their wheelchairs, steadying their backs. Others watched over children, as parents sparred with airline personnel over prices and hidden fees. Still more held bags and sweaty hands, cleaned floors, and translated dialect into English and English back into dialect... I wondered if the humans, the one unaccompanied, were aware of how well we Companions™ were represented, or if most of us went unnoticed.

When my turn finally came, I handed over my documents and saw that the man behind the security desk was not a man at all. As he inspected my passport, his eyes moving with inhuman speed, I started to feel static hives crawl up my body, like a malfunction in my code.

Would he alert Companion LLC?

Had they already notified the authorities, warning that I might try to leave the country?

In the end, there was nothing to worry about. The Companion™ didn't even scan my passport, though he did for everyone else.

It was a wondrous thing.

Inexplicable really.

In Dublin, I walked down cobbled streets, always looking over my shoulder for Companion LLC's repossession agents. I kept a mental log of everyone who passed by—the man with golden teeth, the boy with two popsicles held in one hand, the woman walking in bare feet... If I saw anyone more than once or if they seemed to be following me for more than a couple blocks, I quickly changed course—a serpent diving under the brush.

After one such escape, I ducked into an antique bookstore. Inside, the shelves were lined with first and second edition copies of Joyce, Lavin, Rooney, Barry, and Wilde—each one priceless. The clerk looked at me through rounded spectacles, wonder spreading like flames across his face. It was a horrible, alienating look. I wasn't sure what gave me away—maybe the way my skin caught the light or how my mouth moved while the rest of my features remained unnaturally still. Likely, it was something even more subconscious, an instinctive recognition of the uncanny written all over my face. And, in an instant, he saw me for what I was—inhuman.

I remember thinking, Why don't I just let them take me?

Dubliners seemed to unanimously hate the rain. Whenever someone realized I was foreign, they would apologize for the weather, like the skies were their wayward children, like their bad parenting was to blame. And yet, everyone seemed to love the rain's effects. The precipitation fed the land, it could not be denied. And, they were proud of their grassy fields that burned with the green of a neon sign and fed their wandering, spray painted sheep; the same sheep that, in time, became the lambs that dressed their plates and gave the wool for their knitted sweaters; and they screamed and sang and drank and sweat and crowded in happily, like sardines in a can, when a downpour chased them into Temple Bar pubs in the not-so-late afternoon.

I followed the traffic into The Quays, ordered my Guinness, three euros, paid in coins, watched the bubble cascade, one of the purest examples of gravity-driven hydrodynamic instability, and held my glass like I really would drink the beer inside. Till that day, I had never had a drink of any kind. Companions™ might have the necessary orifices and organs for consumption and digestion, but we can sustain ourselves without food or water, and I generally preferred to do so to avoid the indignities of waste excretion.

Just then, a young man—shaved head, flat capped, straddling a bench—leaned into a microphone and gave his voice over to the crowd. Between songs, he asked for recommendations from the audience, and they rebounded with names of old folk tunes: *Star of the County Down*, *Dirty Old Town*, *The Auld Triangle*... He knew them all and played them as if they were his own.

"It's dark, but it won't kill you," said a man next to me at the bar. His accent, like mine, was distinctly not Irish. He crushed consonants against vowels and swallowed whole syllables as he spoke. His eyes didn't stand still, and he wore the foam on his lip with surprising dignity.

I could see he was sweating. There was a line of still droplets poised along his hairline. Hendrick had hated how sweaty he always seemed to be. With his permission, I had downloaded an expansion pack—six hundred dollars, one kilobyte—that allowed me to cool him down with columns of chilled air released from my every pore. Without thinking, I did this small service for the stranger. To my surprise, he didn't look relieved, but grimaced and shivered, not knowing why he was suddenly so cold.

"I'm letting it settle. I read somewhere that's the proper way to drink it," I said.

"Let it settle, fine. Don't let it go flat."

He was not Hendrick. He didn't sound like him, didn't look like him. But I felt the urge to listen. I was so hungry for someone to tell me what to do. So, I drank.

The beer was heavy, the bag of my stomach swelled with liquid and gas, and yet my head felt light, a helium balloon held to my body with nothing but a string. We talked for hours without learning anything of substance about the other. Mostly, we exchanged little bits of local knowledge we'd accrued during our visit.

"You have to see some hurling while you're here. It's all swinging sticks and bare knuckle brawling. The Irish are mad for it. Little kids, toddlers even, run down village streets, holding their hurling sticks like it's their fifth limb."

"It must be dangerous."

"That's the whole point."

It was late. 02:45:05 IST, 9:45 EST. This was always the time when Hendrick and I would make our seamless transition from the sitting room to the bedroom. He never had to ask. I could read the want in his eyes, the tension in his cheeks, and the eager posture of his hands. Even in this foreign context, in a bar with no American facsimile, I couldn't stop myself from following this routine. I reached for my new friend, whose name I hadn't yet learned. Hand on top of hand. I could feel his heartbeat through his skin. It was noticeably slow and calm—one beat per second. His eyes followed my gesture, his brows raised to full height, and all his harshness slipped from him like rainwater down a drainpipe. In an almost whisper, he said, "Oh we don't need to do that," before ordering us another round.

The next morning, I almost missed my flutter bus. Luckily it was running later than I was. The bus itself was a chimerical thing—made from pieces of many old vehicles, the invention of someone with an eye for scrap. On the outside, you could see the bulging lines where steel was welded to steel. They looked like the metal equivalents of raised scars across skin.

I took a few steps back as the bus's hummingbird wings settled, then stilled, and its metal doors folded inwards. A heavyset pilot, with pigtails the color of wet clay, stumbled out. She took my ticket, but barely looked at it, choosing to eye me instead.

"You traveling alone then?" she asked, like I was a lost kid. I guess, in some ways, I was. John's brain had been damaged in the accident, his memories completely unsalvageable and untransferable. So, unlike other Companions™—many of whom believed themselves to be the person they replaced—I always knew I was just an imitation, and could only access the memories made with Hendrick since my manufacturing, making me just ten years old.

"Yes, it's just me."

I took a seat by a window in the back. The onboard bathroom was to my right, reeking and ripe, so I closed my nasal passages, widened my larynx, and breathed in only through my mouth.

The bus rattled and burped and hissed with every movement. But once it got going, pushing off the ground, wings flapping to a blur, the bus slipped through the air with the grace of a newly minted airship with smooth titanium skin and an engine made of pure gold.

Hendrick had described at great length his time in Kinnitty—a small village in the dead center of the country. It was the last, extended time he had with John before his accident. Tragically, it was also the time when Hendrick had decided he wanted to spend the rest of his life with him. But when I saw the village for myself, it did not match the picture Hendrick had painted for me. Its classification as a "village" did imply a diminutive quality, and still I felt like it may be too small to earn even that title. There were two pubs, a sandwich shop, and not much else. It was cute and quaint, but not remarkable, and I worried that coming here by myself was a huge mistake. At least I was able to lower my guard, knowing this was the last place Companion LLC's agents would come looking for me.

I checked into my room above the Slieve Bloom Pub—seventy five euros a night—and was greeted by a young woman with cat-green eyes and a calming demeanor.

"Just so you know, there will be a hen-do in the pub later on. If they're making too much noise, give us a ring downstairs."

"Oh, that's fine," I said. "I don't want to ruin their fun."

"I know these girls. 'Crazy Colleens' we call them. You couldn't ruin their fun even if you tried."

I threw my bags down by the bed I wouldn't use, and despite the dark clouds in the sky, set out for a long walk, through the narrow country roads, towards the Slieve Bloom Mountains. I was still following a directive, trying to find the spot from the picture I had taken from Hendrick's office. I didn't know what I'd find there, and yet I believed that there was something to find.

The roads were beautiful. Farmland everywhere. Border collies running circles round herds of sheep in the distance. With each blast from their owner's whistle, the dogs changed course, and the sheep followed suit. It was a marvel, watching this three-link chain, living things driving one another like they were gears in a machine, or semi-sentient insects responding to stimuli.

Despite the fact that it was my first time in the Irish countryside, and only my second time outside the Refederated States, I was confident this place had gone unchanged for some time. Everything seemed older than old: limestone walls that predated famines and regime changes, industrialization and the technological revolution. It was arresting.

I sat down on a piece of stone that had fallen away from one of the walls, and then had a truly profound moment with a cow. It crept up from behind me, sequestered on the other side of the stone divide. It had the gold hair of a lion, with a rebellious teenager's floppy haircut. Its mouth moved in circles, a swirling washing machine, slowly chewing as it contemplated me. The rest of its pride soon followed, so that eventually, I was confronted by six fully grown bovine—each weighing in at approximately three hundred twenty five kilograms. They watched me with their onyx eyes, expectant. They wanted food. Something other than the perennial ryegrass beneath their feet.

Over the course of their short lives, they must have built up a Pavlovian response to the presence of a man in this spot.

A man.

I remember blushing. I'm not sure if my face turned red, but my head felt distinctly hot. This was hardly the first time on this trip I had been mistaken for a human being. Even when I was with Hendrick, and in public places, he often asked me to pretend to be just another man. His closest friends, many of whom had also been friends with John, had known it was just a ruse, but I was a good enough actor to fool waiters and shop clerks and even a few newer acquaintances.

This encounter with the cows felt different though. Animals, of the non-human variety, always seemed to have a sort of sixth sense when it came to me. Cats arched their backs, dogs' tails stood straight, and rats paused their grubbing to hiss in my direction. But somehow, without even trying, I had fooled these cows. They believed I was a man, just like any other, just like the farmer who came round to feed them hay, or barley, or whatever qualifies as a bovine treat. And a kernel was born in me, something akin to but smaller and more hesitant than hope, and I started to wonder if there had been some wisdom in Hendrick's plan after all.

My journey through the mountains to find Hendrick and John's spot was waylaid by torrential rain and lightning. I tried hiding under trees, using my absolutely-not-waterproof jacket as a makeshift umbrella, but the storm was relentless and eventually, I had to run back down the mountainside the same way I had come, stepping on many large mounds of wet cow manure as I went.

At this point, drenched as I was and rather covered in shit, I no longer had eyes for the beautiful countryside, the inquisitive cows, and historic walls. Instead, I fixated on the ground. I had failed to find Hendrick and John's spot, and had little hope of ever finding it. Ireland's 32,595 square miles had seemed so small at first, especially when compared to the States' 3,809,525 square miles, but the Slieve Bloom Mountains and their many trails had taught me otherwise. It would take months, even years, for me to explore every path and peak. And surely by then, Companion LLC's agents would have already tracked me down, broken me down to bits, and turned me into someone else entirely. It was one of the lowest moments of my existence. The first time I had ever failed to fulfill one of Hendrick's directives—even if this one was loosely construed.

Though the entrance to the pub was clearly marked, I picked another door that led into the same building, thinking it would give me direct access to the lodgings. Instead, I walked into a room filled with women of varying ages, each wearing pink bunny ears and a shirt that said, "Slag" in bubble letters. They took me in, wide eyed, and surprised. Before I had time to truly process the scene, a woman in the back screamed, "Are you the stripper?"

    I cringe now, thinking about how close I was to ripping my clothes off, mounting the table, and gyrating with reckless abandon—giving these women the show I thought they wanted. How dumb and addled was I to think there was any world in which they had been serious, that they would think a Companion™ like me, drenched to the bone, covered in mud, was there for their evening entertainment? Lucky for me, I hesitated, and before I could make my mind up about what I should do or say, the room broke out into hysterical laughter, one woman laughing so hard that she rolled right off her chair and onto the carpeted floor. A little boy then burst through the door that led back into the pub, racing around with a toy flutter bus in hand, making engine sounds with his flapping lips.

    "Oh God," I whispered under my breath, as I imagined the trauma I would have wrought if that boy had witnessed my misguided attempt at striptease.

But the women were generous, and told me to freshen up, and join them for a drink at the bar.

"We're singing karaoke later on," slurred one of the women, who winked at me about three different times, alternating between her left and right eye as she did.

I did not go to karaoke with the Crazy Colleens, though I could hear the sounds of their drunken, gleeful singing through the building's thin floors. Instead, I stood in my room, listening to the storm and its rage. I was shrouded, not by night, but by a malaise that worked heavy on my head and chest in equal measures, stuck thinking of Hendrick, his hands, and his voice, wishing that my protocols would reset, that my mind would drift off into that promised, pure, peaceful white.

Suddenly, there was a knocking—a closed hand rattling against wood. It took me time to react and understand that the sound meant that someone was looking for me. I opened the door slowly and was met by four sets of bunny ears perched on one ginger-haired head. The face beneath the mane was flushed, elastic, slightly transparent, with wide pores, obviously young.

"You shouldn't be alone up here," she said, wedging herself between door and frame as she did.

"I'm sorry. I'm tired from my hike," I explained.

"You don't like to sing?"

"I can't sing. Or... not well."

My voice was John's voice, raspy, inflexible, always searching for pitch. And still, Hendrick would have me sing arias to him before bed, fully knowing I couldn't reach the high notes.

"Oh, you can sing. All of *you* can sing," she insisted.

She stepped into the room. I could've stopped her. I wanted to. She was small and wiry. But she walked with a kind of confidence that, in that moment, seemed irrepressible.

"Let's make a memory."

Her hand rested on my chest—one hundred twenty heart beats per minute.

"I'm sorry, I don't understand."

But I did.

"My mom says I'm seeing things. I'm not seeing things. Am I?"

"Tell me what you're seeing."

"Linda agrees with me. She says Shane won't mind. He says, 'it's not cheating if it's with another girl' and you're not even that."

She pulled me onto the bed with her, pushing the covers off the side with her feet, wrapping her arms around my neck, touching me as if both of our bodies belonged to her.

I extended my stay in Kinnitty—two hundred twenty five more euros spent on room and board—returning to the mountains whenever the weather allowed. I summited many peaks, and compared the view to the one in the photo, but nothing matched. It's as if the mountains had shifted in the intervening years, like waves on top of water.

During my hikes, I caught myself thinking back to my night with that particularly crazy Colleen. I felt angry and confused and stricken and sick, which was strange—at least for a Companion™ like me.

Hendrick also never asked permission. Hendrick also felt entitled to me. And, whatever his feelings for me might have been—projected or real—I had loved him completely. Over the years, however, as my programming has slowly loosened its iron grip, my feelings for Hendrick have become more confused. There is still love. But also resentment. And jealousy. And so much rage.

In the end, I was forced to give up my search for John and Hendrick's spot. The wind turned thief and stole the photo right out of my grasp. I watched, speechless, as it fluttered down the mountainside, consumed in a sea of trees.

Or was that not what happened? Did I let my grip loosen? Did I want the photo gone?

That night, the photo returned to me.

My eyes were open. I was on my feet. And I was keenly aware of my surroundings—was grounded in it. Still, the wood floors, the plaster on the walls, the ticking clock above my bed seemed tender, made of the soft fabric of dreams.

I felt haunted. I stuffed shirts and pants into the gap under the door, socks into cracks in the molding, trying to plug up any hole through which the memory might creep. And still, it made its way inside. Each time I saw it, the back of the photo was adorned with Hendrick's scrawl, a new, impossible instruction.

"Grow ten feet tall."

"Spin the world the wrong way round."

"Change the course of five rivers. Then change them back."

The hallucinations continued like this for days, never loosening their grip. And I relived my failures again and again and again. Eventually, the woman who worked the front desk, the one with cat-eyes, came to check on me, and I think it was her presence that seemed to finally snap me free.

"Are you ok in there?" she said, through the walls.

It took me time to find my voice, and, when it came out, it sounded weak and raspy.

"Yes. Thank you. I know I owe you for the last eighty six hours and forty two minutes."

"Oh, yeah, don't worry about that. The Colleens are gone, so we have a bunch of empty rooms. Do you need anything? New sheets maybe?"

I looked at the bed. The sheets hadn't been touched since my last visitor had left. And, for the first time, I longed for the lost hours of sleep—something that was completely beyond me.

Eventually, I sought out the coast—where the world seemed to end.

It was no easy feat getting from a nowhere place like Kinnitty to Galway, the country's famous western pole. And it was only after I took a local cab, to a flutter bus, to a Magna train with only standing room available, that I disembarked in the city center. I had left my luggage in Kinnitty. I don't know why, except for the fact that clothes and toiletries seemed suddenly irrelevant to my existence.

Head bent, I stormed through the city's small chaos. I walked down crowded quays, under the legs of stilt-standing knife jugglers, passed teenage street musicians playing 20th century American hits. I ignored the draw of the Companion™ cafes, where beings like me gave themselves over to new masters every day, and avoided looking at the many old Irish people, made of old Irish stock, who contemplated their Guinnesses with grave sincerity.

I didn't care anymore if Companion LLC's people were following me. I would let them take me. But no one grabbed me hard by the arm or pushed me into the back of an unmarked levo-car or shot a static dart into my neck. And I realized that, in the grand scheme of things, Companion LLC didn't care about me; I was just one wayward star in a galaxy of billions.

After twenty minutes of hard walking, I made it to Salt Hill—a stony promenade that walled the land against the sea. Sand whipped through the air as the tide came in and, though I tried to keep my lips shut tight, I could feel salty grit under my tongue and between the ridges of my teeth.

"I thought about walking into the lake outside my grandfather's estate with stones in my pockets. If it was good enough for Woolf, then it must be good enough for a nobody like me," Hendrick had confessed, during one of the many sessions in which our roles seamlessly shifted—him becoming the patient, and me the unlicensed, untrained, but deeply sympathetic psychoanalyst.

"I had such a flair for drama back then. No, I don't think I was ever serious about the idea. And my mother, God bless her soul, was still alive. It would have killed her. I've thought it over, years of just thinking it over, and I eventually concluded it would have amounted to murder. The funny thing is she's been dead for eight years, and I'm still not doing it for her sake. Isn't that strange? Johnny, what do you make of that?"

There, on the beach, I was contemplating the same sort of drama. Filling my pockets with stones, and walking into the Atlantic. It was my whole reason for leaving Kinnitty and coming here. The lakes and ponds of Kinnitty wouldn't do. Too small. Too shallow. Over time, the stones might tumble free from my pockets, and I might resurface and be revived. No. I would need the assurance of the Atlantic, where I could be lost and left.

The world, however, seemed hellbent on distracting me from my objective with tedious little nothings: seagulls milling through piles of seaweed, seeking out morsels to fill their bellies; a man, lying on his side, under the winderbreaking stone wall, carving an elaborate dragon out of sand; a boy and his mother sifting for shells; a ferris wheel churning couples and singles and children and families who all shared the same want for the view from the top; a weed breaking through cracks in the cement promenade, blooming like a flower, not a nuisance at all; gusts stealing hankies from the hands of the old, ice cream from the young; men drinking; women drinking; lovers fighting; violins crooning through the open doors of restaurants and public houses and open apartment windows; a dog standing on the beach's edge, undecided, 'shall I jump in the water or run away?' He ran away at first, retreating to higher ground, but then capitulated, diving head first into white licks of foam and tide.

It was never ending, bombarding, this senseless show, and I couldn't look away.

THE FMMLADE

R.S. Morgan

"Lordy, lordy, Frankie boy, you're on your wrinkled fanny." Tony Twist and his smirking horse face swung into the chair next to my boiler room desk. "I thought you'd be hopping around, flapping your arms, all nervous and jerky. Word is, that Silicon Valley ghost talked to you."

"A ga-ga-ga-ghost?" I asked, light and loose, as if I had enjoyed his prank.

I had not.

I tapped the ash from my cigar into my coffee can ashtray, took a long leisurely pull, and then blew a string of smoke rings past his ear. I hung the final skunky loop on his nose.

I hadn't gone through life being the butt of jokes. And I wasn't going to start now. I waited until the smoke ring on his nose dissolved then I locked eyes with Twist. I had him pegged as a lame joker who'd back down and leave me alone once I let him know I wasn't going to put up with his nonsense. But Twist didn't retreat. He turned in his chair and flattened his hands on my desk and leaned towards me and glared at me as if I was a fly caught in his web and he was going to slowly and soberly pinch off my wings. My throat dried up and when I swallowed it felt like I had drunk my coffee can of ashes.

Twist was trouble and while I was no stranger to trouble, age had mellowed me. And even if I desired to go back to my throw-the-first-punch days, I was no match for him physically. He was young and rangy and had the broken-nosed look of someone who had survived his share of sucker punches. Thrived on sucker punches. The luck of the Irish: I was trapped on the graveyard shift with a psycho rent-a-cop. Still, I knew I couldn't back down. Letting him win our staring match would make him meaner.

"So, Frankie boy, I'm curious about this ghost. This man-made ghoul." Twist's cruel eyes continued to bore into me. "Isn't some whack job genius who, ah, 'checked out' rather abruptly haunting this high-rise roach palace? Barking out names, scaring the help, I hear."

I pointed towards the ceiling directly over my head without breaking eye contact. "See where that water pipe goes through? See the gap around it? Wouldn't it be the simplest—and dumbest—trick in the world for someone to stretch out next to the pipe and holler down?"

"Good golly Miss Molly. Frankie is cranky." He showed me his boxy teeth then leered. "And I know why. You miss your BFF Paulie—"

"That's enough. I'm done playing." I pushed the hot end of my White Owl halfway to his face. "Look, if you wanted to make me jump, take the Lord's name in vain, your prank worked. Good job. Don't do it again. I'm assuming you never knew I had a heart attack. Now you do. No more startle games. I'm fifty-eight years old. Too old for games. Also keep in mind that I need seven more years for a retirement decent enough to keep me in high-end cat food. And if you're slow on the uptake, here's the translation: the job market's tight for stationary engineers my age with nicked-up hearts, I'm going to be here for a while, and I'm going to do whatever has to be done to assure my time at work is as pleasant as possible. And while you're a kid still living in mommy's basement, I'm married, I have a son and daughter older than you, I'm a veteran, and I'd like you to show a little respect." I pulled back my cigar. "Let's get along. How's that sound?"

"Just say it, Frankie." Twist set an elbow on my desk, leaned his cheek into his palm, and drooped his eyes and mouth into a pouty jackass face. "You miss Paulie Wallie. You two were having quite the bromance. Maybe more than a bromance."

I blinked. Even rolled out a soft and astonished chuckle. Then I leaned back in my swivel chair and took another unhurried pull on my cigar and knocked lazy smoke rings towards the ceiling. The taunt about Paulie McManus being any kind of soul mate was idiotic. Although I was always polite to him, would even nod and smile when he stopped at my desk to drone away in his lifeless monotone, Paulie was a short and chubby sleeping pill and our most profound interactions began and ended with chats about the weather.

As for Tony Twist, he was throwing everything at me, seeing what annoyed me. The "Silicon Valley ghoul." My "bromance, maybe more than a bromance." Both succeeded. Yet it was overkill. He had me at the first "Frankie boy."

I initially wasn't upset when McManus was laid off last month. When the Hotel Buffalo became the Buffalo Office Building— the BOB—the lawyers and the other shysters had to be out by 11:00 p.m. Without hotel guests and with the doors locked, there wasn't any need for a night shift security guard. CCTV and window and door sensors were all that was needed in a locked building. In fact, at first, I was glad to see him go, as McManus had mastered the art of being effortlessly infuriating. Leading his long parade of annoying habits was his moist clacking, as if an eel lived in his mouth. He'd lean across my desk and while he was scrutinizing my crossword puzzle for mistakes, I'd tense up as I waited for the eel to wake up then try to get comfortable in one cheek then the other.

McManus' last day on the job was also the last day for the people connected with the Hotel Buffalo. Out the baroque hundred-year-old revolving door went the waitresses, the girls clerking the registration counter, and the taxi drivers hanging out in the lobby. I didn't think it would make much of a difference to me. I've never been all that social. When the building still had hotel rooms, I'd stroll through the lobby on my way to the fan rooms and if McManus was around and my tolerance for the swish and loll of the eel was adequate, I'd say a few words to him then maybe I'd say hello to the vixen checking in the guests and try to sneak a peek down her blouse. But that would be about it. I'd never spend half the night gabbing with the cab drivers and coffee shop waitresses. So it surprised me that after they were gone, I missed them. But I did. It was lonely and, yeah, a little scary being alone on the graveyard shift.

"Yeah, Frankie boy, you miss Paulie Wallie and...you're afraid of me. I can tell. You're a lousy actor. Don't quit your night job."

I leveled my head and looked at Twist. Page two of the Bible states it isn't good for man to be alone. Words of wisdom. But Twist showed me there are worst fates than loneliness. I knocked my cigar ash onto my desktop and backhanded the ash into his lap.

"Oops," I said.

At first, I didn't know what to feel when, a week after McManus was let go, Twist began visiting me in the boiler room. Half of me was happy—initially—because I wouldn't be all alone through the night but my other half was angry because of the rotten trick I felt the owners played on McManus: They packed him out the door with the rest of the hotel crew because he had eight years seniority and was above the entry-level wage. By hiring a new man at the bottom of the pay scale, the owners saved a few nickels. Considering McManus was a capable employee—too much of a dullard to take the occasional on-duty snooze—I felt replacing him was unnecessarily cheap.

But that's business. I've known for a while that a fellow might get trampled if he gets between a businessman and a nickel. Still, I was a little surprised. The owners had always been decent. Not as heartless as some of the other local outfits or all of corporate America. I decided to give them the benefit of the doubt. Maybe switching from a hotel to an office building really busted them and they needed to cut costs every place possible.

Twist looked down at the gray ash crumbling on his polyester pants then looked up again. We narrowed our eyes at each other then I knocked another ash on my desktop. I let it slumber.

"Hey, here's another idea," I said. "I know how to get along with people I don't get along with. I just stay away from them as much as possible. Let's try that."

"That's probably a good idea because rumor has it..." Twist arched an eyebrow. "You're about to see a ghost. And I'm not talking Casper. Uh-uh." His eyebrow looked like an electric eel, poised to pounce and jolt, that had slithered out of McManus' mouth. "This one's a bad ghost."

Seven years ago, Dimitri Glasnovich, the "smartest man ever," came to town to give a talk at the University of Buffalo. Dimitri was a dot.com billionaire who made a sweatless fortune on graphene. He cashed out for $20 billion and at the time of his murder he was deep into his life's work: eternal life.

"After all," he explained. "Einstein said if one could travel faster than the speed of light, one would go back in time. Is life after death that much more of a stretch? It is not."

According to Dimitri's equation, tidy up Einstein's Theory of Relativity, then add one-part photon dilation, two parts string theory, puree with quarks and some parallel universes and "I'm back." Even his fellow eggheads had no idea what he was talking about.

While crunching the numbers on life after death, Dimitri married porn star Rosita Coxxx. Rosita didn't have the usual porn pedigree. She wasn't pulled out of a tilted single wide. Didn't have a creepy stepfather. Rosita was the spoiled brat daughter of a Silicon Valley venture capitalist and, until she became a professional sword swallower, a straight A student in physics at Stanford. She wasn't the intellectual equal of Dimitri. Nobody was. But she could at least ask some of the right questions.

Dimitri and Rosita were in the celebrity spotlight almost as often as the Kardashians, yet not for being barely dressed and looking bored. Their faces—often his sported a black eye or a puffy lip—were splashed all over the internet for public displays of disaffection. The explosions were usually about his infidelity. He liked the ladies and the ladies had twenty billion reasons to like him back. And while their prenup agreement to have an open marriage looked good on paper, the lawyers hadn't run it by the green-eyed monster living inside Rosita's head. They'd be at a swanky restaurant, Rosita would get a text, pull up a video of her husband lipping it up with a starlet or being twerked by a barmaid, and the crystal and the sea bass would start flying.

Rosita began to accompany him on his lecture tours and Buffalo was the end of the line in more ways than one. As usual, on stage at Shea's Buffalo, Dimitri asked for volunteers to die. There was nervous laughter. Then silence. Dimitri paced the stage, his head down, his black-velvet Moses beard gently swaying, his hands clamped behind his back. Eventually, he turned to the audience.

"No volunteers?" He asked, spreading his arms. "No one want to die tonight? Then live forever. To sleep then, I guarantee it, to dream. Yes, yes, science this advanced looks like magic. But it's not." Dimitri, his arms stretched, stood as still as death in the spotlight and stared into the dark and silent audience. "No one? Well, even though there's nothing supernatural about what I'm offering, you're wise to say 'no thanks.' At least for now. Oh, I'm coming back. As some sort eternal entity. I know that. But, as you might have noticed, I haven't taken a swan dive off the Golden Gate Bridge. Not yet. And that's because I don't yet know how the afterlife will be. There are many parallel universes on the other side of death, some naughty and some nice, and I'm not exactly sure how to avoid the hellish ones. I'm working on it but until I solve the puzzle, yes, conscience does make cowards of us all."

Rosita never said what drove her to the end of her line. But twenty-one floors above my boiler room, while Dimitri was apparently contently dreaming of a sun-splashed eternity, Rosita planted a room service steak knife into his heart. Then she called 911.

"I killed him," she calmly said as she waved the officers into their suite. Then, in a very un-Stanford manner, she added, "and he ain't coming back."

I agreed. Many intellectuals, however, did not. They insisted Dimitri was going to return as the "first man-made life-after-death entity." The fmmlade. Whatever. And whatever variety of ghoul he was supposed to be, weird science or old school, I was not shocked when, low and behold, small hours sightings followed his murder. Never, however, did Dimitri Glasnovich appear to the man who was at the Hotel Buffalo the most during the small hours. Me.

The night after I locked eyes with Twist, I heard my name barked out again. A deep garbled slow croak. It was time to fire off the boiler and I was bent over checking out the draft linkage. Hearing "Fraaaaankie booooy" shouted out unexpectedly startled me again but this time it didn't cause me to worry about my heart. I was too angry for that. I had jerked up after hearing "the fmmlade" and had banged my head on the burner port.

I turned around and slowly scanned the boiler room. My head stung and rage bubbled in my stomach. I wanted to rub my coconut but I wasn't going to give Twist the satisfaction. I didn't see him right off and he could have played hide and seek a bit longer if he hadn't laughed; a high-pitched grating put-on shriek of a laugh. Twist was squatting alongside the pipe rack, yelping and pointing at me. If Twist insisted on playing games, I had planned to talk to the owners and try to get him fired. I hadn't planned on any physical confrontation. But I was too hot to be sensible. I walked over to the opposite side of the pipe rack, yanked out a two-foot length of one-inch galvanized, dangled it by my side, and circled over to Twist.

"Get out and don't ever come back. The equipment here's too delicate and too dangerous for a horse-faced halfwit to be around."

The laughter and pointing stopped immediately.

"What? What did you say, what did you call me?"

He slowly rose from his crouch and with controlled brutality in his eyes, he swaggered towards me. Fright drained my anger and I momentarily froze in place. I hadn't been in a fight for twenty-five years. Never wanted to fight again. Twist raised his hand and swung it as if he was going to slap me but stopped inches before my face. I unfroze and backed up, terrified that as soon as he was done toying with me, he was going to knock out my teeth. Maybe stomp me to death. I shouted at him not to come any closer. Squeezed my fear into the pipe in my hand. Threatened him. Even whispered an unhinged prayer to the fmmlade to swoop down and scare him off. Yes, I was that desperate. Then, short of breath, I pleaded with him.

But Twist apparently not hearing anything. He and his merciless eyes backed me down the dim, narrow dead-end corridor between the boiler and the chemical room. Through a village of spider webs that had been undisturbed for months. A mouse squeaked away. I huffed at him to leave me alone as I stumbled through the rat's nest of chains near the musty end of the corridor and bumped into the back wall. But the raw-boned lunatic kept on coming. Twist raised his hand and started to swing it again. I howled as I raised the pipe over my head. I swung wildly. In panic. Just wanting some room. Not wanting his rancid breath in my face. His skull made a dull, almost pleasant, thud when the pipe caved it in. Twist dropped down in a pile at my feet.

 I tried to let go of the pipe but it was as if it had become part of my hand. As if my hand had enough sense to wait and see if I'd need it again. I waited, panting, with my back tight against the moldy bricks. My heart was trying to thump its way out of my chest and I felt like a man who would never completely catch his breath or have a calm heart again. Yet eventually my breathing and my slamming heart came under control. And I grunted hello to the runner-up to my wildest night ever.

 My eyes stayed fixed on Twist. I prayed he'd twitch. Prayed he wouldn't. He never moved. I stepped over him, rested the pipe by the firebox door, then slow and shaky, I squatted down; half expecting him to lash out at my throat, and checked his pulse.

 Feeling no pulse, I knew what I had to do. What choice did I have? He never touched me. If I went to the police would they believe self-defense? And even if I was eventually cleared, I would undoubtedly be out of the BOB forever. Out of *all* work forever. And equally as bad, if not worse, would be the grief and humiliation my family would suffer. My hangdog face in the *Buffalo News* and brazen high-heeled beauties from Eyewitness News shoving microphones at wretched me, the wicked old ogre who bludgeoned to death a fine young psycho.

 I stood up and went about my business. I was gradually becoming calm. My decision had been made. There was a way out. I unbolted the firebox door then swung it open and tossed the pipe inside. Then I went for Twist, dragged him by the shoulders to the open door, and jammed him into the firebox.

I shut and bolted the firebox door then went to the front to the control panel and switched on the programmer. The induced draft fan whirled to life as it began purging the boiler. I lit a White Owl then went back to the fire door side of the boiler and closed my eyes as I leaned against the wall. I opened them a moment later. Stupid. How could I be so stupid? I hadn't taken the time to put Twist directly in front of the flame path. Curled up by the firebox door, he wouldn't disintegrate completely. To see if he was possibly in far enough, I stepped forward and lifted up the viewing flap. I slammed it down immediately and let out a wheeze as I lurched back and thumped into the wall.

Twist's face was squeezed into the viewing flap and we nearly touched noses.

"Frank? That you, Frank?"

I said nothing. I just stood there, pressed up against the wall, and listened to Twist's trembling breathing. I told myself to walk to the front of the boiler and switch off the programmer. Yet I didn't move. If I let him out, I was certain a man as mean as Twist would make me pay a price. Either he'd attack me or try to have me arrested. Maybe both. There would be no forgiveness for sparing his life. And his big and hateful mouth would also bellow to the world about how he had been wronged, piped and stuffed into a boiler by a dangerous nutcase. A fiend who should be locked up forever. And I would no longer be local news. I'd be the internet creep of the week.

Still, the situation wasn't impossible. If he called the police, I'd deny all his accusations: "I put him inside of where?" And even with all that CSI wizardry, I doubted the truth could be proved. Additionally, I hadn't any police record and a perfect work record. Now that he was alive there was only a slim chance I'd lose my job. Most likely, after talking to the owners; after they weighed my eighteen trouble-free years against his unbelievable story, they'd fire Twist. Most likely. As for him attacking me, yes, I was afraid of him. I was frightened he might even try to kill me.

Still, I felt I could back him off with a pipe. He had to be groggy. He had to also be as scared as I was and I was fairly certain I could bluff him away until he was given the boot.

But what if I was charged with a crime? All the misery that would flow from that. Or what if the owners decided to let him stay? Then I would have to face him five nights a week, terrified of when and how he'd take his revenge. Or what if the owners fired *me* instead? I decided leaving the programmer on was much less troublesome. Yes, the time for turning back had passed. I stepped back up to the viewing flap and jerked it open. Twist squinted into the dim light and focused his pleading eyes on my face.

"Yeah, it's me, Tony. Listen, don't worry. I'm going to get you out. I guess I went a little off the chain. I'm going to switch off the boiler but it will have to go through its pilot cycle before shutting down. Just take two steps backwards so you don't get burned leaning against the bricks. Now put away the long face." I winked, trying to keep it light. As if being trapped inside the hellfire side of a boiler—a crematory—was a big nothing. "Everything will be fine. I'll be right back."

I didn't want him to suffer, didn't think he'd suffer. But I needed him dead. I eased the viewing flap back down, walked to the front of the boiler, and strung some smoke rings until the purge cycle was about over. I then walked back to the side of the boiler and lifted up the flap. Twist had stepped back. His knees were shaking yet he flashed his Clydesdale teeth and gave me a scared, jittery smile. Just to let me know, I imagine, we were still friends and we could later laugh about my better prank over beers.

Then the pilot light clicked to life and lit up the firebox like Hell's waiting room and his skittish smile twitched away and he no longer seemed concerned about clinking pint glasses as the fear inside him bubbled to the surface. His eyes grew big and round and he began to frantically lick his lips and jerk his head back and forth between me and the two slender lines of blue flame snaking towards him. No. Not a trace of a smile. He was terrified. And so was I. My heart felt swollen enough to explode. My blood pressure no doubt high enough to blow out my eardrums. My mind shrieking. Shriller and shriller each passing second.

"Frank, this is pretty weird. I'm scared, Frank. And, ohhh, my head. But, hey, forget about my head. I deserved it. Now you sure everything is going to be all right?"

"Worry not. You'll be leaving the boiler very soon." I puffed on my cigar and tried to look benevolent. While no doubt looking like Lucifer eyeing up his newest arrival. Because I felt like a demon. Was I really going to do this? I had an Irish temper. Knew anger and sudden violence. Yet I wasn't a cold-blooded killer. "This will all be over in ten seconds."

That wasn't the kind of reassurance Twist wanted to hear. He cupped his hands around his mouth and screamed for help. Me? I began to whisper. I wasn't even aware that I was murmuring out a countdown until Twist became silent and turned towards me. His face, backlit by the licking pilot lights, initially asking the question. Hoping. Pleading it meant the right thing. While all the time knowing it meant the worst.

"No, Frank. No. You can't. I don't want to die."

I suddenly felt strangely calm. The calm before the firestorm. Then when my countdown reached zero, certain this unreal madness was about to become very real, I whispered, "May God have mercy on your soul."

And as that executioner's farewell was still hanging fresh in the stale air, the two main valves swung open and a wide surge of natural gas punched through the burners and by the pilot lights and the concussive blast lit him up and corkscrewed him down to the brick floor. Knocked him unconscious, I believed, and I mouthed a prayer of thanks. He hadn't suffered. But then he scrambled to his feet and ran towards me, his polyester uniform melting on him like shrink wrap, his hair a smoldering halo, and his final scream ringing in my ears. I slammed down the viewing flap. Next to melt, I knew, was going to be his face. I spared myself that.

Tony Twist died like a witch burned at the stake.

Yet I remained eerily calm as I threw the rest of my cigar into the flame. I had done what had to be done. I wasn't going to lose my job. I wasn't going to be attacked by Twist. Nor was I going to be arrested for murder. A man can't be arrested without evidence. And I was certain the evidence would soon be transformed into ashes and sent up the smokestack to float with the pigeons and issue no complaints.

Then all became strange.

Twist had told me he lived with his parents. They, I was sure, would report him missing and the police, learning he had gone to work and never come home, would have some questions for me. I wasn't particularly worried about talking to a detective. I'd simply play the part of the concerned yet clueless co-worker. Tell the detective I had seen him at work. Didn't know what he had done or where he had gone after work. And that would be it. Still, I wanted to get the police visit behind me.

Then all became clear.

Three sleepless days later, I went to the front office before my shift to ask about some bearings I had ordered, detoured to the afternoon manager's office, and stuck my puffy face inside his doorway. I wanted to see if the police had made any inquiries. How incompetent could they be? The afternoon manager, the pie-faced nephew of one of the owners, swallowed down his mouthful of potato chips then waved me to his desk.

"Good evening, Mr. Buchheit. Sorry to trouble you but I haven't seen that new night security guard for a while." I tried to sound and appear apathetic. "Did he quit? Are you going to hire anyone else?"

"Do you know something I don't know, Frank?" Mr. Buchheit laughed politely as he eyed up his tasty fingers. "After we let McManus go, we never hired anyone else." He considered his fingers for a few long moments then looked back up at me. His round face was serious and critical instead of amused. "Is there a problem, Frank?"

I felt lightheaded. Like my head was going to float off my shoulders. I silently stared at Mr. Buchheit for a while. "No, no. Nothing," I eventually said. "I meant to say were you going to hire anyone after McManus."

I knew. Knew what had happened. Knew why a detective hadn't questioned me.

Mumbling a good-bye, I drifted out and walked downstairs and exchanged some dazed small talk with the afternoon engineer. He gave me his usual cheerful thumbs-up sign as he back stepped towards the stairs. I waited for him to disappear around the corner then I wandered to the front of the boiler and stopped in front of the narrow, dusky dead-end corridor and peered down it.

"Oh, Frank. Frankie boy. I've been waiting for you. Patiently waiting for you to figure it out. Come in. We have unfinished business. Yet before that, allow me to thank you. Without guests, you were the only game in town. And you, Frankie boy, exceeded expectations."

I stepped into the corridor. Tony Twist, his arms crossed, was leaning against the moldy end wall. We studied each other as I slowly advanced and I was so intent on him, I put my face into a newly slung spider web. I slapped at the sticky web. Twist was amused. He laughed pleasantly.

"My man is afraid of spiders but not afraid of me, the fmmlade. Well, I suppose that makes sense, as I can't attack you. Truthfully, I can't even so much as tweak your nose."

"I want this resolved." I continued to inch forward until I was a yard away from him. "Now."

"My, you certainly are a brave man."

A dim light formed around Twist then began to gently pulsate. Twist transformed into a cloudy then distinct Dimitri Glasnovich. He smiled at me as he moved his Old Testament beard to the side and showed me his fatal stab wound. It opened like a tiny mouth and an apparent shower of blood blasted me. I didn't move.

"Nothing brave about it because you're nothing," I said, stepping even closer. "Oh, you're more vivid than any ghost I've ever heard of. But you're not flesh and blood. Boil out all the special effects and all you are is that too-real nightmare that dissolves after a few deep breaths. And I agree—you can't hurt me. Hey, appear all you want. I don't care." I reached out put my hand through the fmmlade's head and swirled it around. His face broke up like a murky kaleidoscope then I pulled out my hand and chuckled as I leaned against the boiler. "Excuse me for being happy but I feel almost giddy. I didn't kill a man. After I roll out of here, I'm due for a rare morning drunk. Then I'm going to sleep soundly. Nothing but blue skies and white clouds rolling through my dreams. So if you have any more parlor tricks, let's have them. I'd like to get them out of the way."

"Ah, Frank, Frank, Frank. Parlor tricks? I rather like that. No, you didn't kill anyone. But you tried. Someone must pay. Because, while there are many doors on the other side, murdered-too- soon me—that bitch—picked a door to a bad neighborhood. It's not nice and I'm no longer nice. There's no mercy in my forever. No forgiveness. No Jesus. Just meanness and payback. And you know what they say about payback. Sorry, Frankie boy, but it's not over."

Dimitri blurred and throbbed and swelled up into Tony Twist. A furious Tony Twist. His head then morphed into a stallion's head. He snorted at me. His pitiless eyes studied me.

"What's wrong, chuckles? Suddenly you're not so bubbly. Your old heart switch gears? Why? I can't hurt you. I really can't. Physically. But the mind is much more vulnerable than the body. All one has to do is find the tender spots. And, fact is, there's more tender spots than days in your pathetic life. For instance..."

Twist reached out his hand and looped his fingers around my belt buckle. He pulled his arm back but his hand remained. It dangled from my buckle. Then it evolved into a spider. A spider as big as a large fist. A swollen white sack of eggs drooped from its back. It looked up at me; its face that of Tony Twist, and worked its pincer jaw back and forth. I then felt its dangling back legs needling through my pants and puncturing my testicles. I groaned and swatted at it as I slumped down but it was too quick; or the illusion was too quick, and it snuck between my shirt buttons and began scurrying up my chest. Little stilettos pierced me as it ran. My shirt bulged and I frantically cried out for mercy as I punched at it. The spider popped out of my shirt at my neck then scrambled and sprawled onto my face; its eight powerful legs crunching into my skin; its breath hot and rank; its sharp jaw snapping at my eyes.

It jammed its egg sack into my pleading mouth. I gagged. The sack burst. I wildly grabbed the hairy body of the spider and tried to rip it free. But the legs were dug in too deeply. They remained embedded in my face while the body ripped apart. Warm intestines oozed and spurted onto my face. I rolled onto my stomach. Thousands of baby spiders; babies twice the size of full-grown spiders, were in my mouth and hurrying either down my throat or out onto my face. Spinning webs across my eyes and ears. Nesting in my hair. I scratched and slapped my face and threw up. Then the hallucination melted away. Still, I continued to claw and pound at my face.

"Frank? Frankie boy? I hate to disturb you but it's over. No, that's not really true. It never did happen in reality so how can something be over that never was? Of course, those welts and scratches on your face are real. Ah, I'm no philosopher. You figure it out."

I lay flat on my face. My vomit-tasting mouth was squeezed shut and I was trying to hold in my sobs. Moments before, I was happy. Relieved I hadn't killed. I began to crawl away but then collapsed. There was no use in running. There was no escape.

"Oh, c'mon, Frank, things aren't all that gloomy. Fact is, you're awash in decent options. Unlike Elvis, I can't leave the building. You could just up and quit. But with but a mere seven years to go until cat food heaven, quitting would be a pity. Be tough on you and your family. Old and poor is not the way to go. No, you won't quit. You'll stick it out. And, as long as you don't die of a heart attack, I promise to keep your years interesting. You seem to respond nicely to bugs. Tomorrow we'll start with bloodsucking millipedes the size of hot dogs swarming you. Parlor tricks like that."

I closed my eyes as I sat up. I whispered a prayer. I prayed I had lost my mind. Then I slowly opened my eyes and, as I feared, as I knew, the insanity was not inside me. Twist, relaxing against the back wall, smiled at me.

"I'll tell you want, Frank. Softie that I am, one more murder—a real murder this time—and I'll go away for a while. Let's just consider that little deal with Twist inside the boiler a dress rehearsal. Oh, I'm not going to ask you to put your mother in there. I'm not particular. But, you know, I'll bet you have a plan already. I'll bet you're going to bring your victim in through the oil delivery door. There's no CCTV or sensors there. Sure, you're conflicted. You're no killer. That's no line you want to cross. But bottom line, Frankie boy, it's time to cross that line."

If I was a better man, I would have taken my chances with this mad scientist of a spook, this elaborate shadow. But I was just an ordinary man. An ordinary man whose heart was going to burst. An ordinary man whose mind would not stop howling. Twist transformed back into Dimitri then the fmmlade throbbed into a dim light then flickered away. I pulled my knees up to my chest and began to cry. I cried about what had happened and what I was going to do. I told myself no. Yet I knew. I just wanted this howling inside my head to stop as soon as possible. As easily as possible. A half hour? An hour? I don't know. But after some amount of time, I stopped blubbering and wiped away my tears. Then I stood up and walked back to my desk. Everything was so jumbled. I didn't want to think. I just did it. I picked up the phone.

Paulie McManus was thrilled. The eel clacked. He was coming right over.

I DON'T DO DRUGS: I AM A DRUG

Curt Tyler

A long queue to the dentist is the last thing you want to see when a toothache is killing you. *It's going to be one of those days*, I thought as I was squeezing my way through the swarms of dental casualties that had flooded the corridor, to reach the reception desk, which appeared at a distant horizon of the waiting room: a lighthouse to the crew of the ship lost at sea in the storm.

"Can I help you?" the receptionist asked.

I mumbled back that I needed a tooth to be removed. My words painted confusion on the receptionist's face so I opened my mouth and pointed at the culprit: the second molar on the left side of the upper jaw. Confusion turned into disgust, but the demonstration served its purpose. I filled in the form and collected my number: 666.

As I was squeezing my way back to the end of the queue, I thought of what constitutes consciousness: the electric impulses between neurons. I imagined I could see these tiny lightning bolts through the transparent heads of the people around me: buzzing cobwebs, floating above their necks.

I sat down and contemplated this carnival of dental atrocities. So much pain in such a small place.

I took out my mobile phone to occupy my mind with anything but the merciless inflammation devastating my jaw. As I scrolled through a social media page, a black-and-white photo of the surrealist painter, Dani Salvador – playing with his thin and long moustache, grabbed my attention. Placed below, his quote: *I don't do drugs. I am a drug,* painted an elusive smile on my face.

Suddenly, a sharp pain in my nostrils made me forget about my aching tooth. Salvador's moustache had sprouted out of the screen and gone for my brain! In agony, I stood up, distraught, bellowing like a deer in mating season, with my mobile dangling from my nose on those swirling tendrils. The pendulum of madness! When the painter's facial hairs reached my frontal lobe, the time and space melted like the watches in his painting. I fell to the floor. My soul, fed up with my nastily itching brain, left the convulsing body and rushed up like a helium balloon, caught by the ceiling. As if gravity reversed direction, up was down and down was up. But left and right remained the same.

A distant voice in my head shouted: "Get him out! Get him out! Now!" The balloon burst and everything turned black, apart from a small red light in the bottom left corner that enticed me with the scent of Italian fresh-tomato sauce. I swam towards it in a frog-like style and squeezed myself through to the other side.

"Mr President, he's back," said one of many apron-wearing men to a bearded guy sitting behind an impressive desk with American flags behind. I knew this face! It was Philip X.

Dickson, a legendary sci-fi author! Tied to a chair, gagged, bristling with plastic tubes that seeped varicoloured potions into and out of me, all I wanted was to clarify the meaning of the last sentence of his most famous novel, *Ubiquity*. But the muzzle didn't let me produce anything better than an unintelligible mumble.

Dickson approached me and said: "Try harder! You're the last hope to stop this **BLOODY INVASION!**" He didn't bother to remove the gag, so I just nodded. "Dr Salvador," he looked towards the Spanish maniac who brought me there, "hit him with another impulse."

The painter, apparently also a doctor, pranced towards me, swinging a curly cable. He stuck it into my left nostril.

"What are the levels of the telepathic-precog aura?" President Dickson asked.

"Sixty point eight ubiks per cubic metre," replied Salvador.

"We have to make sure it works this time! Turn it up!" the President ordered, pointing a remote control at me.

"It might be dangerous."

"I know, but we have to take the risk. Give him one hundred, now!"

A drop of sweat ran down my nose. A laser beam flashed. A blink of an eye followed. An infinitesimal piece of space-time later (or further?) my head was a star with its own planetary system. The rest of my body had ceased to exist. Effectively, I was just a ball of fire. I heard a crunch. The surface of one of the planets cracked in a cloud of dust, pushed from the inside by an enormous hand. A tree-legged, four-armed and two-headed beast got out and shook the soil off its wrinkled body. Drops of sweat froze under its hairy armpits. Each head had its own eye: only one, bloodshot, purple irises, slightly convex, goofy-looking. Each mouth drooled with thick saliva. The creature stretched out one of its arms into space. Its massive fingers grabbed the planet's pink moon. The beast made a series of swings like a cricket player and threw "the ball" towards me.

"No!" I shouted. The moon travelled at an impossible speed. I didn't have time to close my mouth.

I heard a click. A laser beam flashed. A blink of an eye followed. I found myself in a dental chair.

"Your jaw will be numb for at least two more hours. If you feel pain, take paracetamol. This should help. You're free to go unless you have any more questions," said the dentist. I didn't reply, perplexed by the unexpected turn of events I'd just experienced. When my tongue located a gap in the lower row of my teeth on the left, a temporary unification of dream and reality into a higher reality (a surreality?), struck me as a plausible explanation. But I couldn't be sure of anything, including my reasoning.

When I returned home, still dazed and confused, I sprawled on the sofa and lit up an irresponsibly well-deserved cigarette.

I switched on the TV. Neither the reality show nor the football game seemed interesting at all. My belly growled with hunger and anger so I went to the kitchen. As you have probably guessed, the fridge was as empty as my stomach. Apart from five jars of Polish mustard I buy in bulk.

There was a leaflet on the floor. *Pizza Hot Delivery 24h. It must've fallen out of the bin.* I browsed through the menu while dialling their number.

"Hello, it's *Pizza Hot*, how can I help you?" said a woman on the phone.

"Hi, I would like to place an order, as you may have guessed."

"Yes sir, I've guessed that. I've also guessed what you want to order."

"What is it?"

"*Shrooms Extra Large with Spaghetti on Top*, and coke. The mobile network distorts your aura, so I'm not sure if it's Diet Coke, Coke Zero or the regular one."

"Maybe Zero."

"OK."

"I don't need to give you my address, do I?"

Her tone of voice changed dramatically. "Of course not! I'm a well-trained precog!"

"I'm sorry, I didn't mean to—" I was embarrassed.

"You people think that anyone could do this job, right?"

"I'm sorry."

"You should be! You know I could put you on the list!"

"No, please. Don't do that!" The last thing I needed was to be on the fucking list. I was hungry. I needed food. "I'm sorry. I really respect your profession."

"Alright. It's your last warning. Our driver will knock at your door three times."

"What's the password?"

"Murmurations. It'll take thirty to thirty-one minutes."

I returned to the room and stared out the window at the trees bent by the wind saturated with the piss of autumn weather.

Knock, knock.

I glanced through the peephole. There was a man with a pizza. He wore a baseball cap; *Pizza Hot* was written on it; it felt legit but I asked anyway, just in case: "What do you call a large group of birds, usually starlings, flying and changing direction together?"

"Murmurations."

I opened the door. The delivery guy smiled at me. "*Shrooms Extra Large with Spaghetti on Top* for you sir."

"And my coke?"

"She said you wanted zero coke."

"I think she meant Coke Zero.'

"Well, too late."

"Well, forget about your tip then."

"What tip?"

"I don't know."

"Neither do I. So, bye, enjoy your meal."

I put the pizza on the table in the living room. The smell wafting out of the box was mesmerising but one thing was missing: Polish mustard! So I quickly took it from the fridge. Back in the living room, I poured the mustard onto the pizza and spread it over the round surface with my bare hands. And I licked my fingers, purring with pleasure. *Like ambrosia.*

I lit up another cigarette. Halfway through the third puff, I turned on the news channel.

Shivers ran down my spine when a disturbed speaker announced in a trembling voice: "BREAKING NEWS! Vlad Dracula wins the election in Romania. Fresh-blood markets are in turmoil."

Hearing that, I recalled President Dickson's words: *You're the last hope to stop this **BLOODY INVASION!***

My mobile phone rang. It was a private number. At that moment I finally grasped the ambiguous ending of *Ubiquity,* Dickson's most famous novel: *This has only just begun.*

FARAWAY, NEARBY

Wayne Kyle Spitzer

Lightning flashed, doing its white-hot paparazzi dance, and Tika jumped — not in reaction to the too-close strike, but to the pale, gaunt ghost of her own reflection.

I'm dead already, she thought.

Then the darkness returned, and she was able to peer outside again, though there were only two things within eyeshot which provided any interest: the **DISABILITY CLINIC** sign below, banging back and forth in the storm, and the leviathan weeping willow just beyond her window, the branches of which scraped the glass.

She'd gotten nothing but bad news all day, and her head was a cacophony of voices: *No, I'm afraid the procedure out of*

Germany has encountered some setbacks ... Yes, some of the test subjects have regained mobility ... No, I don't think it will become viable in your lifetime ... Yes, the tumor has grown ... Yes, you'll die if it isn't excised ... No, I'm not going to lie to you about the odds. We're looking at a fifty-fifty chance of survival ...

She realized she'd been toying with a length of her hair, twisting it, tighter and tighter, about a frail finger. She let it unwind, watching it unravel by the dim glow of the nightlight.

She'd been a perfect student through grade school, high school, and most of art school. She'd been a perfect catch for Gus, her first love. Sam, her second. Alex, her third, and Russ — her last. She'd been a perfect bitch through most of the '90s: she'd drank a lot, been paralyzed from the waist down on an L.A. freeway at 2 a.m., had crawled to and held a stranger she'd been riding (and sleeping) with as he died ...

She was 27 at the time. Now she was 34. Her hair finished unwinding and lay still.

At least it's still gold, she thought.

"Okay, Tika ..."

Maggie entered the room, carrying a dinner tray. "Or should I call you *Hell on Wheels* — suppertime."

Maggie was the night nurse. Everybody said she looked exactly like Whoopi Goldberg, and she did. She was popular with the inpatients and always seemed comfortable in her skin.

"I'm not hungry," said the young woman. She stared off blankly. "And I'm not on wheels."

She flinched as Maggie kicked one of the bed's rollers. "Your chair may be in the corner — but you've still got wheels."

Tika gazed out the window and said nothing. She gazed at the willow tree.

"Poor thing," said Maggie.

She switched on the overheads, causing the tree to be lost behind a mirror-image of the room. Thunder cracked and rumbled.

"The docs might be able to cut out that tumor, Tike, but they can't prescribe for you a will to live ..." She sat down the tray and turned to the wall calendar; its days were checked off up to October 15th, with the 17th marked OP DAY in bold, black letters. She checked off the 15th. *"You've got to do that. Those who won't, don't come back from major ops."*

Tika looked at her wheelchair, which sat in the far corner of the room. The spokes of its wheels gleamed mockingly: they shimmered. Like a necklace, she thought. Or the chromed rims of a crushed sportscar in the L.A. heat.

"Maybe I don't want to come back," she whispered.

Maggie lifted the lids from the entrees. "Yes you do, sweetie. You just don't know it yet." She started to leave, then paused in the doorway. "On or off?"

"Off," said Tika.

Maggie clicked off the overheads. "Now eat," she said, and left.

Tika sat in the darkness, thinking of her wild days, of losing her family and her innocence and her legs to the wind, of bedsores and spasms and shitting her pants, of hospitals and clinics.

When she awakened, there was a fly buzzing about her Jell-O and the ice-cream had melted. The storm was still on, but seemed farther away — so much so that she could hear the solemn ticking of the wall-clock. And something more: a squeaking sound, like the protests of a wheelchair too long neglected. It was coming from outside her room. It was coming up the hall.

She looked at the doorway.

Sure enough, an old woman in a wheelchair muscled her way past, skinny, ashen elbows working. It was a comical sight, frankly. *Slow down, you old bag,* Tika wanted to call out — and almost did. Then the squeaking stopped, abruptly, and the old woman backed slowly into view again. She looked at Tika.

The younger woman looked back. Between them, up on the wall, the old IBM clock ticked.

The resemblance was uncanny. Both women had long hair, though the younger's was blonde and flowing, like lemon molasses, and the older's was thin, platinum, flyaway. Both were skinny. Both had blue eyes, fine features, were gaunt as castaways, and —

Suddenly, the crone was rolling, *charging,* Buchenwald elbows pumping rust-spotted wheels, a hand like a dead tree branch reaching out, groping, flailing, batting away Tika's I.V., tumbling her saline bottle which shattered against the blood-red tiles ...

Maggie was at the nurse's station, filling out her log, listening to Peter, Paul and Mary singing "Puff the Magic Dragon," when the buzzer went off. She peered down the hall over her reading glasses; the light beside the door to room #22 was blinking rhythmically. *Tika,* she thought, alarmed by the uncharacteristic timing — uncharacteristic for this visit, anyway — and hurried toward the room.

Maggie heard Tika protest as soon as she turned on the overheads — a good thing, because it let Maggie know she was all right. She clicked them off immediately and went to her.

"What is it, hon?"

The young woman's face was whiter than usual, and she was trembling. She looked at Maggie forlornly. "Bad dreams," she said. "Again."

"Ahhh ..." Maggie drew a cup of water, handed it to her. "The iron-sided crone back to haunt you?"

Tika nodded, solemnly, and took the cup.

Maggie looked down at her, hands on hips. She sighed. Appearing to collect her thoughts, she pulled up a chair. "I'm gonna tell you a bedtime story," she said.

Tika turned away, embarrassed. "Maggie ..."

The problem with Maggie was, she didn't just look like Whoopi Goldberg — she acted like her sometimes.

"*Shhht!* You need this. Now, when I was a kid, I had what you'd call a secret friend. A ghost, actually ..."

Tika looked out at the great willow tree — and for the first time, noticed a strange anomaly: a weird bulge in one of the branches farthest away, a bulge about the size of an apple barrel. She squinted, studying it. Lightning flashed whitely as if to assist her.

"... her name was Angel. And whenever I'd get depressed, or was feeling sick, I'd hear a tapping at my closet door, which was Angel wanting out —

Tika spun around. "That's horrible!"

"Oh, you don't know the half of it! She'd knock and knock and knock — until finally I had to crawl out of bed and let her out. And then she'd pinch me so hard I'd scream — and she'd run back inside, giggling. And I wouldn't see her again all that day, but it didn't matter, because I'd be so angry at her for getting me out of bed that I'd forget all about being depressed, or even sick, and pretty soon I'd be out playing again."

Tika grinned in spite of herself, then lightning flashed outside, and thunder cracked, and she sobered instantly.

After a long pause, Maggie asked: "Did you have a secret friend?"

"Not a horrible one like that ...!"

"So you did have one?"

Tika sighed, relenting. She squinted her eyes, thinking. In her mind's eye she saw the bristles of a paintbrush slathering green paint on a dark blue surface. But the thought seemed to evaporate as quickly as it formed. "I — I don't remember."

"Well, think about it awhile." Maggie tapped her temple: "This is mightier than the scalpel. Not all miracles are miracles, sweetie. And not all Angels are angels."

She gathered up Tika's untouched tray and dimmed the nightlight. "And since you're not going to eat, why don't you try resting your eyeballs again."

Tika watched as she pulled the privacy curtain around its track. "Maggie?"

The nurse paused, facing her through a part in the curtains. "Why do you fuss over me so?"

There was silence as the woman looked at her in the dark. "Because it's important you survive this operation," she said. Her tone was uncharacteristically grave.

Tika swallowed dryly. "Why is it important?" Her voice sounded small, vulnerable. "Beyond plain old human compassion, of course —?"

Maggie seemed circumspect. "I don't know. It just is." Her expression lightened: "Night, Love."

And she left.

Tika settled back in the darkness. Rain drizzled down the window; lightning flashed somewhere nearby. She closed her eyes, resting them. Before long she'd begun to drift off.

There was a sudden, blinding flash, followed immediately by an explosion of thunder. She opened her eyes with a start and looked outside.

The giant willow tree stood its ground. Rain fell upon its branches and pelted against its deformity. The wind was blowing, she could tell, causing loose leaves and pine needles to take to the air. The hairs on the back of her neck began to tingle.

A bolt of lightning struck the deformity, showering sparks and snapping branches. Tika leapt. For a moment all she could see was a snapshot of the bolt, supered over everything, burned into her retinas. The thunderclap rattled the pane violently. When her vision cleared, she thought she saw the bulge in the tree's blackened trunk glowing within, throbbing bluish-purple.

The nightlight flickered beside her; she gazed out at the smoke-shrouded willow, transfixed.

Maggie was nearing the end of the corridor when the lights flickered and went out — and the emergency lights came on. She paused, looking around: The building had gone completely dark. She turned and rushed back.

The curtain around Tika's bed was drawn back, and Maggie poked her head in. "You okay, kiddo?"

Tika turned around, looking at her — but hardly seeing her. She gave Maggie an absent "thumbs up."

"Good. I don't imagine we'll be down long." The lights flickered back on. "Well ... See? Get some sleep, hon. We'll mind the store."

She left. Tika stared after her a moment, then turned back toward the window.

Now that the smoke had cleared, she saw that the bulge had burst open, and was hollow. Reams of tree sap dribbled from its fracture. She stared at it as piano music tiptoed up the hall — Maggie's radio, no doubt — resonating eerily amidst the sterile walls. Thinking she heard the ghost-voice of Karen Carpenter — what were recordings if not the voices of ghosts? — she noticed something different about the willow tree. Something other than the weird bulge, now split open.

It was an odd configuration of branches, some thick as a person's arms, others thick as legs. Had those been there before? She was pretty sure they hadn't. She noticed there were unusual masses of vegetation growing from them; in addition to strands of weeping willow leaves, there were flowers, ferns, lilies, mushroom stools —she *knew* they hadn't been there. Taken together, the branches almost formed a human shape — with shaggy shoulders and a mane of green hair — in profile. But since when did trees grow —

Suddenly the shape turned its face to her, opening its eyes, and Tika shrieked.

Maggie stopped abruptly, hearing Tika scream. Thunder rumbled and the lights in the corridor flickered. She whirled around and ran toward the room, grabbing a candy striper along the way. "C'mon," she said.

Maggie batted the privacy-curtain aside, rushing to Tika, while the candy striper checked the IVAC unit.

Tika shrieked: "There's something out there!"

"What do you mean ..." Maggie turned, taking notice of the doorway. "Something out there?"

"Out *there!* Right outside the window! Look!"

Maggie glanced toward the pane. "Tika, I don't —"

She paused, staring out. Then she went around the bed and *peered* out, her nose nearly touching the glass. The candy striper joined her.

They looked out at the willow tree. It was a veritable still-life save for a few blowing branches. They looked at the storm. They looked at the clinic's sign, banging back and forth in the wind. Maggie pulled the curtains closed.

She turned to Tika, who met her gaze, then glanced at the candy striper. "That's all, Lynn. Thanks."

The orderly left. Maggie regarded her patient as the storm rumbled outside.

"What was I supposed to see out there?"

Tika watched her, and there was a long silence. "A — a creature," she said. "It — it looked like a vegetable."

The two looked at each other. After a tense moment, both started chuckling.

"A vegetable, huh? What kind?"

Tika tittered. "All kinds."

"More like a soup, then ..."

They laughed. Gradually, the silence reasserted itself. Maggie brushed a lock of hair away from Tika's eyes. "Look, doll," she began, "what's going on here is obvious. Old crones in wheelchairs, monster vegetables — it's all the same. You're seven years in the chair and the thought of 70 more really freaks you out. But you've got to ..."

Tika glanced at her wheelchair as Maggie talked. Her smile started to dwindle.

"... have hope, babe. You've got to believe. Not in some miraculous cure-all, but in *belief* itself. 'Cuz belief, like hope, is something real. It's physical. It keeps you alive because it *makes life worth living."*

Though Tika was frowning, she continued: "And your body recognizes this even if you don't. That's when miracles can happen, though they're not really miracles at all. If you have hope, you have life. And if you have life ... you have hope. Do you see?"

Tika suddenly felt very tired. She thought of skinny-dipping with Alex in the summer of '87. She thought of dancing at the Viper Lounge in 1988. She thought of flowing gowns and lingerie and jogging in Fenrow Park. She thought of love, and of sex.

She exhaled. It was all so far away ...

"Those are nice words, Maggie. They really are. But I have neither of those things, and know it." She paused.   "I ... I think I'd like to be alone now. Thank you."

Maggie studied her.

"Okay, hon," she said after a while. She glanced at her watch. "I'll be going off here in about ten minutes, so, get some sleep ..."

There was a *squeak* at the window and Tika jumped.

Maggie shrugged. "Just a branch, sweetie."

She headed for the door — and bumped into an entering security guard, who flipped on the overheads.

He asked: "Everything okay?"

"We're fine," said Maggie. "Thanks."

She flicked the overheads back off and left. The thirtysomething guard glanced into the room at Tika, and caught her eye. She and he had one of those little romances — the kind which was bound to happen in some other life, some other dimension, but probably not in this one. Tika liked him, even if he was wearing a nametag in his thirties. Maybe he went to college by day — a girl could hope, couldn't she?

She waved. He smiled, and was gone.

So far away, nearby, Tika thought.

She settled back, staring at the ceiling. The wind blew; thunder rolled. The squeaking sound came again: *Squeak — sqik — squawk ...*

She studied the ceiling, which was cracked and a little yellow, like an elderly person's skin. She saw the door to the room in her mind's eye: it swung open, revealing the old woman in the wheelchair.

She shifted her gaze to the curtains.

Squik — sqwork — squeak ...!

Her brow furrowed. Again she seemed to recall paintbrush bristles, delicate strokes — the slathering of brown and green on a dark blue surface.

KNOCK-KNOCK!

The glass rattled.

She jumped, startled. Then, suddenly furious — she didn't know at what or whom — she reached out and grabbed the edge of the curtains, yanked them down. Lightning flashed and thunder boomed.

There was nothing there except a fog of breath. And the word:

"BOO."

Tika stared at it, bewildered. She refocused her eyes on the willow tree.

The creature poked its head and shoulders out and "pooh-poohed" her, holding its thumb to its nose and waggling its fingers. Her heart skipped a beat. Then it crawled out from behind the trunk, its tail uncoiling, and crouched on the branch nearest the window.

Tika swallowed hard.

It stared at her through the rain, elfin yet ape-like, with pointed ears and a tapered brow, flared nostrils, a pug-snout. Its amber-resin eyes twinkled. It cocked its head, loosing raindrops from its mane of willow-vines, and grinned.

She almost screamed, but didn't. Instead, she gazed deep into its eyes — and into herself, for she could see her reflection in the rain-drizzled glass. It was superimposed upon the beast by the nightlight's glow. Her face was flushed with warm blood from the pounding of her heart, and alive with fear. She cocked her head, recalling smears of green and brown ...

There was a glint of silver and her eyes darted to it.

The creature's hand was palm up and something shined as it closed its fingers. Tika watched as the thing put the object in its left hand, made a fist, then turned its right palm up. There was nothing there. Then it turned its left palm up also — but again there was nothing. Tika lifted her gaze to its face as it reached first behind one ear, then the other. Still no object. Finally, it shrugged its leafy shoulders and stared at her.

She felt a sudden coolness behind her right ear, as if metal were touching her skin. She reached up, slowly. There was a glint as something fell, tumbling into her lap. She looked down.

It was a little, silver unicorn. Her eyes widened. *My God,* she thought. She picked it up, amazed, then turned to look at —

The creature was gone.

She peered out the window. As she did, she heard water dripping behind her, and was overwhelmed by the smell of the outdoors, only here, in her little room. She froze: it was the smell of wet bark and of soaked moss. It was the smell of moist, black earth. Her eyes shifted slightly — there was a strange, coiling appendage reflected in the glass. It undulated out from behind her slowly, accompanied by a sound: a bizarre, croaking purr.

It was the creature's tail.

She whipped her head around. The thing sat upon Maggie's chair, perched almost regally — like some kind of monstrous housecat. There were termites crawling in and out of its ears, and earthworms winding through its hair. It loomed over her close as she looked up — slowly, nervously. She was trembling noticeably.

It stared at her intensely, its head at an angle. Tika saw its pupils widen and constrict. It reached out suddenly, splatting its palm against her face. Its long fingers curled about her head. For Tika, everything went black, moist, silent ...

She was in a blue room. She didn't know how long she had been there, or even where *there* actually was, but it was a silly question, anyway. *She was there.* A little girl of about nine was sitting on the floor, on her knees, at the far end of the room. Tika couldn't tell what she looked like; the girl's back was turned toward her. But she could see what the girl was doing clearly, even if she couldn't see the results. She was painting something on the wall.

Tika walked toward her. There were no clocks, no windows. The silence was surreal, but soothing. The place had the ambience of an empty hotel; she sensed there were many corridors just out of sight, and many, many rooms. But she didn't wander. She moved to within a few feet of the child, and stopped.

She admired her a moment, watching how the light played over her hair, setting it to shine. The little girl continued to paint. Then, as if sensing a presence, she paused. Her paintbrush wavered in midair. She turned, slowly.

Tika looked at her. The girl had long, golden hair, pretty, blue eyes, a thin face with pert features. She wore a medallion around her neck. Tika lowered her gaze: it was a little, silver unicorn.

The girl smiled, making eye contact.

Somebody's little elf, thought Tika. *A long, long way from L.A.*

"See my picture?" She stepped aside to reveal her painting.

Tika looked at it: it depicted a green and brown tree against a stormy sky. Clinging to the side of the tree was a green creature, a sort of leaf-goblin, sporting a mischievous expression. Willow vines sprouted from its head and dangled, like the points of a jester's cap. Tika's eyes welled up.

"Do you like it?" The girl wiped her hands on her paint shirt.

Tika looked at her. "Why yes, I like it very much. Does it have a name?"

The girl nodded. "It's a *he*. His name is Sylkk. He only comes when it's darkest."

Tika closed her eyes, smiling. She inhaled deeply. Then she reopened them.

"*Sylkk* ... Sylkk." She nodded, beaming. "That's a nice name. And what ... what is Sylkk?"

"Oh, he's a monster. But he's a good monster. He comes to my window when it storms." Her tone became conspiratorial: "I think God sends him."

Tika tilted her head, puckishly. "But you said he was a monster ..."

"He is," said the girl. "But he's an angel, too. Only grownups think all monsters are bad, or that all angels are beautiful."

Tika thought about it. "Or that all Angels are angels, for that matter."

The girl nodded, solemnly.

Tika glanced at the unicorn about her neck. "I like your medallion, Tika."

The girl noticed that big Tika wore one identical to it. "Hey, you've got one just like it!" She sounded persecuted.

"Yes, I do." Tika rolled her own medallion between her fingers. "Shall we see how alike they are?"

She held it out and touched it to the girl's. There was a flash of light.

Tika awakened to sunlight. It was streaming through the window, warming her face. She squinted her eyes, blinked. With a struggle, she lifted her head.

She was alone in the recovery room, her bedside crowded with flowers. Her neck hurt and she laid back down. She stared at the ceiling, which was overcast with balloons, and tried to recall the dream she'd been having. She vaguely recalled an anesthesia mask being lifted away, bright surgery lights shining down. She'd been surrounded by figures in surgery scrubs and masks. They'd looked like Martians, she remembered, and grinned. They'd all started clapping and slapping each other on the back.

She rolled her head on the pillow, looking at the flowers. Someone had left her a red rose, she noticed. It was wrapped in silk and had a little envelope leaning against it. The envelope read, 'From Your Secret Admirer.' Her security guard, maybe?

An almond-skinned hand reached into view, setting down a bowl of Jell-O and a spoon. She turned. It was Maggie, dressed in day-clothes. Tika had never seen her out of uniform: the lady looked like a million bucks — tax free. She sat in the chair next to the bed.

"I hear the operation was a success," she said, and beamed.

Tika beamed also. "I guess it was," she said.

"The docs are even throwing the word 'miracle' around." Maggie's eyes seemed to sparkle.

Tika looked at her, keenly, as if to say: "Touch'e!"

The nurse winked. "I'll see ya tonight, kiddo."

She stood up, patting Tika on the shoulder, and headed for the door. Tika sat up on an elbow. "Maggie ..."

The older woman paused, turning to face her.

"Thanks," said Tika. She struggled to find the right words. Thanks — for opening the door."

Maggie looked bewildered for a moment. Then she smiled, warmly, and left.

Tika picked up the Jell-O and spoon and went to work, finding she relished every bite. Aside from the sound of the silverware clinking against the bowl, the room was eerily silent.

She was cleaning up her bowl, head bowed, when something gave her pause. It was as if the room were static-charged, causing the hair to stand up on the back of her neck. Slowly, she looked up.

A woman stood in the doorway. She looked to be about fifty, maybe fifty-five, and was dressed nattily in blue jeans, boots, a fuzzy sweater, and a beret. She was leaning on a pair of crutches.

Tika stared at her. She liked the way the woman wore her hair, which was gold with streaks of gray — cut short, bobbed; it was perfect for her age, and for the shape of her face. Tika figured it was how she might wear her's someday.

The woman moved forward, graceful in spite of the crutches. She smiled beatifically, appearing almost to shine. Tika noticed she was wearing a silver unicorn medallion about her neck. The woman reached the bed, and stopped. She reached out with a liver-spotted hand, which quivered in the empty space between them, and touched Tika's cheek. There was a flash of light.

Tika looked at where she'd stood. There was nothing there.

Knock-knock!

She jumped as the window rattled. She turned, looking out.

Sylkk was perched on the branch nearest the pane, looking in. He reached up and tapped his temple. Then he smiled, slyly.

Tika smiled, too. *Mightier than the scalpel,* she thought.

And then she realized there was nothing there.

She leaned on her elbow and gazed out at the day. Who knew: maybe the events of the last 24 hours had all been in her head. Maybe the powerful medications had made her hallucinate, sending her to an imaginary land faraway, yet nearby. She only knew that they'd succeeded in excising her tumor, that, like the weird bulge in the tree outside — it was gone.

She picked up the little hand mirror by her bed and looked into it. Her color was back, and she certainly didn't look dead. In fact, she felt more alive than ever. She sat it down, looking toward the door. Had that been a vision of herself, twenty years from now?

It had been a vision of hope, she decided. A *Faraway, Nearby*. Something which might not ever happen, probably wouldn't happen, but *could* happen. She glanced at the red rose and the little envelope beside it.

That was good enough for her.

SIGN ON THE DOTTED LINE

David Sheskin

One clear winter evening Mr. Scabs ran a red light. As he exited the intersection he felt a light thumping sensation. Hearing a loud moan he stopped his car thinking that perhaps he'd run down a pedestrian. Looking back he could see someone lying in the middle of the road. Suddenly in a sweat, Mr. Scabs heard a knock on his window. Looking to the left he saw a middle-aged man with incredibly white teeth and lustrous hair peering through the glass. Mr. Scabs rolled down the window to hear the shiny stranger say "You hit a man back there. He's hurt pretty bad and it doesn't look like he'll make it. Since it's such a clear night this whole thing looks pretty bad for you. Anyway you try to play it they'll probably get you for manslaughter. In case you don't know it that carries five to twenty years depending on how the judge takes to you. From where I'm standing you look like a decent sort of fellow who had a momentary loss of concentration. Could happen to anyone. Lucky for you I'm the only one to see this thing. I think I can offer you a pretty good deal and get you out of this mess practically scot-free. The fact of the matter is I got this son who's scheduled to go into the army tomorrow. Joined the reserves so the draft wouldn't get him. He's always been the lazy type who takes to sulking real easy. Well, to be perfectly frank, this whole thing with the army has him pretty upset. His mom and I don't think he'll ever make it as a soldier, so what I've got in mind is that you take the kid's place and I take your place. For you it'll mean six months of active duty and after that five and a half years of Tuesday night drills and two weeks each summer playing war games. It's a damn better deal than serving a bunch of years in prison."

Somewhat startled Mr. Scabs replied, "Well, I don't know."

The stranger, who got shinier by the minute and whose body seemed to be emitting waves of heat, produced a pen and a piece of paper. "It's entirely up to you. I'm not going to intimidate you or anything like that. It's just not my style. Frankly, if I were in your shoes I'd grab a deal like this right away. Let's face it, any way you work it out you wind up going on a trip. It seems to me the army's a better deal than prison. Listen though, I'd like to wrap this thing up right away. I've got a worrying wife and kid waiting for me to come through the front door. Just sign this piece of paper and I'll issue you a uniform and your traveling orders. After that I'll prop myself in your seat and take the rap for you."

Regaining his composure Mr. Scabs inquired, "But why take the rap for me? If you really want to help your kid why don't you go in his place?"

"Never mind that one. The deal wouldn't be much fun if I answered everything."

Mr. Scabs couldn't see himself in the army at his age. He'd managed to evade the service all through his youth and now to get nailed in his mid-forties seemed a bit ironic. On the other hand, he couldn't imagine himself in prison. Interrupting his thoughts, the shiny stranger said, "Okay, let's have your decision. There's a crowd gathering and in a few minutes one of us is going to have to take the rap."

Looking out the back window Mr. Scabs saw a restless crowd gathering at the intersection. Judging from their sounds and gestures he suspected that he'd run down a beloved member of the community and that the crowd was more interested in revenge than in truth or justice. Panicky, Mr. Scabs grabbed the pen and paper from the stranger's hand and scribbled his name on the dotted line. The shiny stranger nodding his approval deftly slipped into the driver's seat, and in the same motion deposited Mr. Scabs outside the car. Extending his hand the stranger said, "Thanks loads. I'll have the kid give you a call in the morning and drive you to boot camp. Your uniform and travel orders are behind that bush across the street." Just as the stranger was about to say something else, the angry crowd rushed Mr. Scab's car and grabbed the man by the coattails. As he was being carried off he yelled back to Scabs, "Take my advice, you'll save yourself a night or two of KP if you get a GI haircut before you get to boot camp." That was the last he saw of the shiny stranger who was hustled into a mysterious looking car that sped away towards what Mr. Scabs imagined was some sort of prison.

Feeling somewhat relieved, Mr. Scabs concluded that he'd probably gotten the better of the deal. Being a man of honor he walked over to the bush and found a duffle bag filled with a uniform and a stack of papers. He swung it over his shoulder and started to walk home.

Arriving at his house in a sweat Mr. Scabs was confronted by his wife who asked, "What took you so long, and what's in that bag you're carrying?"

"I've had some trouble. Right now I don't feel much like going into details. All you've got to know is that I'll be going into the army for a few months. Tomorrow morning a kid will call up and give me more details."

The next morning Mr. Scabs was awakened by a phone call.

"Hello, my dad sent word you'll be serving my army time. Have a good breakfast, get yourself a GI haircut, and say your goodbyes. I'll come around at noon to drive you to boot camp."

As Mr. Scabs gobbled down his breakfast his wife sulked in the living room. After returning from getting a haircut he said to his wife, "I'll be back in about six months. If I'm lucky maybe I'll see you before that if they come up with some furloughs. There's money enough in the bank for you to take care of yourself. I've taken out a couple of bucks for PX money — you know, for cigarettes and candy bars. Don't forget to call my boss and tell him I'll be back to work after I get my military obligation out of the way."

Looking out the window he saw a car pull up and heard the horn blowing. He told his wife, "Well, I guess that's it. I'll see you around."

Hoisting the duffle bag over his shoulder he walked out to the car. Seated inside was a shiny looking lad who was the spitting image of his father. The boy nodded to Mr. Scabs saying, "Put the duffle bag in the trunk. Wipe off your feet before you get in the car. Once you're inside there'll be no smoking, eating or drinking."

Doing as he was instructed, Mr. Scabs seated himself beside the young man. Immediately he felt an unusual amount of heat coming off the youngster's body. In a benevolent gesture he inquired, "Are you ill? I can feel you're hot."

Looking at Mr. Scabs the young man replied, "There'll be no questions."

As the two of them drove along the boy seemed to give off more and more heat. The color of his skin seemed to fluctuate between a hot pink and a fiery red. In a moment of insight Mr. Scabs sensed that maybe he was in the company of something demonic and suddenly began to feel nauseous. Turning to the tight lipped young man he cried out, "I feel sick and I'm going to throw up. You better stop the car and let me get it over with"

Not wanting his car soiled, the young man came to a sudden stop which caught Mr. Scabs so much by surprise that he smashed his head hard against the windshield. He was knocked unconscious and because of this didn't get a chance to throw up.

When he awakened he found himself inside an army reception center. The young man was nowhere in sight. Mr. Scabs was in his underwear seated in a corridor with a lot of recruits waiting in line to be processed. Feeling panicky, he raised himself to his feet and looked for the man in charge. He saw a sergeant at the front of the line and ran up front grabbing him by the arm.

"My name is Scabs and I'm really not supposed to be here. Someone played a trick on me. I'm forty-five years old and there's no way in the world a man of my age can be a recruit."

With a look of sympathy the sergeant looked at Mr. Scabs and said, "Listen fellow, all of you boys feel a little bit homesick. It's only natural. But take my advice and don't make a pest of yourself. There are some people around here who don't like that sort of thing. I'll tell you what, if you calm down, after we get you processed I'll let you call your mom and dad. Now be a smart fellow and get back in line."

"Gee mister, didn't you hear me? I'm forty-five years old and I'm way out of shape. Last night some slicker tricked me into taking the place of his draft dodging kid."

Feeling the need to be firm, the sergeant said, "You're a soldier now mister whether you like it or not. Now, get your ass back in that line or I'll put you on KP for the next two days!"

Just as he was about to protest some more Mr. Scabs remembered how his hands swelled up every time he tried to help his wife with the dishes. He envisioned himself being thrown into a huge kitchen filled with dirty dishes and harsh detergents. Without another word he scuttled back into line.

That evening Mr. Scabs was marched to some barracks with the other recruits. He was assigned to share a bunk with a dour looking youth named Cutter who whose body was tattooed with swastikas and satanic symbols as well as being impaled with multiple piercings. Although Mr. Scabs had never had any contact with bikers or other aficionados of body art, he'd always considered himself to be open minded. Trying to ignore the uncomfortable feeling that had erupted in his belly when he realized he would be sleeping underneath Cutter, he tried making conversation.

"I bet you got all those tattoos to cover up some sort of bad skin condition. Even though I can relate to that, if I were in your shoes I'd of had some doctor clear my skin up using drugs or a laser."

All at once, without warning, Cutter pounced on Mr. Scabs and slashed him about the face with a switchblade. The next thing Mr. Scabs heard was the voice of a young hospital orderly.

"Interesting connection. Rather elementary when you think about it."

A woozy Mr. Scabs asked, "What's that? What are you talking about?"

"Cutter man. They call him that because he always carries a blade with him. Some psychiatrist figured it out after they wheeled you in here."

Mr. Scabs suddenly realized he was in a hospital bed, his face swathed in bandages. Sensing that perhaps the orderly might be able to help him, he said, "Listen fellow, I'm forty-five years old and I really shouldn't be in the army. Some guy I met a few nights ago did a real nasty thing to me and that's the only reason I'm here. You look like a bright kid. Do what you can to get me discharged and I'll see that you get a free college education."

The orderly's eyes lit up. "No kidding mister?"

"I'm an honest man. I don't fib."

The orderly reached under the mattress and pulled out a pen and a piece of paper. "Just sign on the dotted line and I'll see what I can do for you."

Hesitating for a moment Mr. Scabs sensed he'd been here before and figured maybe this time things would work out better than previously and signed on the dotted line. Three days later he was discharged from the army.

That evening he called his wife and told her to pick him and the orderly up at the train station. When she arrived he let the young man sit in the front with his wife. Mr. Scab's told her, "I met this guy in the service. He'll be staying with us for a while and I'll be footing the bill so that he can get himself a good education."

That night while the orderly slept Mrs. Scabs said to her husband, "How can you afford to send that guy to school?"

"I made a deal with him. I signed a piece of paper."

His wife began to sob. After a while she said, "Why is your face bandaged up?"

"I had a little trouble in the service. I don't feel much like discussing it. All you've got to know is that I had a run in with a guy with a lot of tattoos and piercings and because of it I'll have a few scars."

The next morning Mr. Scabs withdrew some of his savings from the bank and gave the orderly $5000 for his first semester of college. The orderly said, "Well, I guess this'll get me through the first few months."

A week later the orderly came by to get more money. Mr. Scab's reaction was, "Gee fellow, I wish you'd try and economize. I'm not a rich man." Mr. Scabs gave the orderly another $5000. When he returned for more money a week later Mr. Scabs decided he had to get out of the deal.

"Listen kid, I'll give you $10,000 and we'll call things even. Does that sound fair to you?"

"No deal. According to the contract you signed you pay all of my expenses as long as it takes me to get through school."

As he heard this Mr. Scabs felt a familiar pattern of heat emanating from the orderly's body. He also sensed that every time he saw him the young man seemed to take on more and more of a shine.

The next morning Mr. Scabs called up the dean of the college the orderly was attending.

"Hello, my name is Scabs and I've got to talk to you about a certain fellow who's going to your school."

"I can't see you now. I'm busy. Maybe I can squeeze you in tomorrow."

"I'm in a hurry and I'm coming to your office. Every minute I wait costs me a ton of money."

Twenty minutes later, rushing up two flights of stairs Mr. Scabs found the door to the dean's office half open. Inside there was a scholarly looking man standing over a woman's body. The man turned towards Mr. Scabs and said, "You must be Scabs. I'm the dean. I had to kill this lady. No sense going over the whole story. All you've got to know is that she tried to blackmail me. Now what's on your mind?"

"There's this guy I promised to put through college. The problem is he's a big spender and I'm not a wealthy man. I figure if we can work out some way you can give him a quickie degree I can get him off my back."

The dean frowned for a moment and said, "Okay, you seem sincere. I think I can help you out. I'll make sure the guy gets a degree. All you've got to do is call the cops and say you killed the little lady on the floor. She had a bad reputation and all. Most likely the judge will let you off real easy. I'd take the rap myself but I've got some pretty important conferences coming up the next few weeks and I can't miss them."

Sensing that he was on familiar ground Mr. Scabs said, "Fine, give me something to sign." As the dean produced the familiar pen and paper Mr. Scabs felt unusually hot. He realized this only happened when he was around certain people. Once again and probably not for the last time he signed on the dotted line.

THE HOLE

Meg Keane

It had just been a crack in the dirt when Peter leaned over the scorched grass, shielding his eyes from the sun. He turned to pluck a stone from the pathway which ran the length of our humble backyard. With the dusty stone in tow, he knelt beside the crack and placed a chalky finger to his lips to ensure I didn't speak, though I hadn't anything to comment, nor the intention of voicing it. We watched as the stone plunged into the dark abyss. Both listening carefully and hearing, well nothing.

"You were breathing too loudly," he said, getting up with a huff to his feet. "I didn't hear it land."

"Maybe it wasn't heavy enough to make a sound, or maybe it still hasn't landed?"

Peter scoffed. No longer did he look at me with admiration, love, or even lust. Those feelings had long faded like the spring breeze and left in their place was the suffocating air of contempt.

"Fill that in tomorrow," he said, gesturing towards the hole. "There's dirt in the garage."

I nodded briefly before trailing him back inside.

The sun was almost setting; it was dinner time. Leftover meatloaf, mashed potatoes, and greens. The steam whirled in the air as I placed the dish down in front of him. Peter jerked his head theatrically towards the arm of the couch, the delivery of his dinner blocking his view of the television. He was watching a show about get rich quick schemes, investments, and how to keep your house in order. I said enjoy, in hope that it may arouse a thank you but he only replied with a tiresome glare.

I ate in the kitchen, over the sink. I wasn't to play the radio when Peter's show was on, so I hummed softly to myself. It made sense to get a head start on the pots and pans before the oil set and grease hardened. The hot water ran into the basin as I scrubbed back and forth; gazing sightlessly into the yard. The light lingered in the summer sky while the night attempted to out it. The crisp yellow grass was motionless in the evening breeze and I awaited the day we could turn our sprinklers back on.

Warm suds ran down my forearms as my gaze fell on the hole in the center of the lawn. Somehow, it looked wider than before.

There had been soil in the garage, six bags of it. Peter reminded me of my task as I rinsed the syrup from his breakfast plate. The water ran hard and fast against the slow-moving liquid. All I had to do was fill in the hole.

The bags were heavy and there was no way of feeding my arms under each sack, so I resorted to dragging them. Pinching the short plastic wrapper between my fingers until my hands burned. The weatherman had insisted there be no hard labor during the warmest hours and to stay inside whenever possible. Though the weatherman mustn't have had a growing sinkhole in his garden, nor Peter to contend with if it wasn't filled. Dust kicked up as I dragged each bag across the balding lawn, creating sandy trails in my wake.

Once the bags were settled around the hole, I used Peter's hunting knife to slice through the plastic. Soil spilled out like entrails from an animal. With much effort, I lifted the soil to tip it into the hole. Just as the dirt began tumbling out, I noticed something. Beside the hole on the bare grass was a stone. There were no other large stones on the lawn and I hadn't dragged the soil over the pebbled pathway, so it had no other reason for being there. The soil bag slumped to the ground, half empty. I plucked the stone from the ground for further inspection. It was smooth, and round and had a red mark on it. Just like the one Peter had dropped into the hole the night before—which was impossible, of course. We both watched it fall, consumed by the darkness. An oddity, I noted but not without simple explanation. Returning to the task at hand, I sliced two more bags open. The dirt burst from the newly opened seams and onto the ground. On I continued filling the hole, though it grew no closer to being full.

The fourth and fifth bags didn't touch the sides. After the sixth and final bag had been dumped, I sat beside the unchanged hole. My hairline dripped and my shirt stuck to my back now slick with sweat. I dropped the stone back into the hole.

The sun was climbing higher in the sky, its first light cascading across our back fence. Soon it would creep along the grass until it reached the house. I got to my feet and brushed my dusty hands on my gardening dress, intent on getting straight into the bath.

When I returned refreshed, the sun was beating down on the house and the breeze had halted. Drops of condensation dripped over the counter as I drank down two cold glasses of lemonade consecutively; though my throat remained dry. Peter would be home soon and the hole was no closer to being filled than it was when he left this morning. The empty bags of soil wouldn't be proof enough that I'd tried, and he wasn't to be reasoned with.

After plating up dinner, he gestured towards the back door with the television screen glare reflecting in his eyes.

"I take it that was taken care of."

I paused for a moment, unsure of how to explain. But when he turned to face me with an accusatory stare I simply nodded. "Of course, darling. All done."

I excused myself to the kitchen and slipped out the backdoor. The skies were still light despite the hour and I was able to navigate my way to the hole. Despite being six bags of soil fuller, it looked wider than before. In fact, it had grown almost a yard in diameter in just a few hours. The dark crevasse had fallen in on itself to create a larger hole. Panicked, I glanced back to see the lamplight and hum of the television still playing in the house.

When I turned back to the hole, I noticed something odd. There by my feet, an inch from the earthy opening was a stone. It was smooth and round with a red mark on it. While I could find explanations for the first time, now it was uncanny. I saw it disappear into the black abyss with my own eyes—how could this be? Uncertain of my next move, I stooped to grab the stone and slipped it into my apron pocket.

"You don't like rocks, I suppose," I said unexpectantly. And to my horror, a gravelly voice responded.

"*Meat.*"

I staggered back from the hole in disbelief, my palms thrust over my mouth to avoid alerting Peter. Then, it repeated itself.

"*Meeeeat.*"

The pitter-patter of light feet sounded somewhere near the surface and quickened its pace as I lurched towards the backdoor. Quickly but quietly deadbolting it shut. There I slid down against the wooden frame so as not to be seen through the glass, and to stop my legs from giving way under me.

"Come in here," Peter called out from the living room.

While unstable, I got to my feet and attempted to act natural; not daring to look back. My hands shook vigorously as I collected his dinner plate from his lap. If he noticed, he didn't comment on it. His eyes flickered between mine and the screen beyond my shoulder.

"The chop is overcooked and dry," he said, folding his arms across his chest.

At that moment, I was relieved to be invisible to him. Usually, I'd apologize, or at least respond to his complaint, but I found that all words had escaped me. Instead, I took the plate into the kitchen, my eyes fixated on the lump of chewed meat in front of me. Steam filled the air as the hot faucet ran. I rinsed the used pans and cutlery, unable to look into the backyard.

Silence fell as Peter lowered the volume during the commercial break. In the soundless room, I became aware of my own labored breathing and the rapid rise and fall of my chest. Convinced of my own insanity, I raised my head to peak through the drapes and steamed-up window. Outside remained untouched and I scanned the lawn until my eyes reached the hole. One brief look before shutting my eyes tight, but it was too late. Imprinted in my vision were two bloodshot eyes peering back at me.

We went to bed as usual, though everything had changed. As I laid awake next to Peter's incessant snoring, I could hear soft groans coming from the backyard. Begging over and over again to be fed. Butterflies swarmed my empty stomach as I awaited sunrise; as if the safety of the sun would protect us.

Morning came agonizingly slow and Peter watched with cautious eyes as I provided his breakfast beside his dinner plate.

"You ain't washed that up yet?" He said, pointing towards the cold meat and limp green beans.

"Oh, I must've missed that one."

I lifted the lid of the trashcan and hesitantly held the plate above it. The soggy greens slid off first but I tipped the plate up just as the meat began to fall. Without thinking, I hid it behind the toaster and set about cleaning up breakfast.

Once he had finally left for work and the greasier pots were soaking, I retrieved the hidden plate and slipped outside.

It was quiet in the yard, as it should be. The early morning sun had not yet reached us, though the clear sky hinted at another insufferable summer day. There was nothing amiss outside, that I could tell. The empty sacks of soil still remained untouched and there was little else to meddle with beyond the skeletal remains of spring shrubbery. I approached the hole but remained at what I considered a safe distance. With arms fully extended in front of me, I tipped the plate and watched the meat slide off into the darkness below. Heatstroke, I was certain that would be the revelation I came to after feeding a hole in the dirt. You hear about it on the news, women do crazy things when it's hot out. I'd laugh about it afterwards.

No laughter came.

What followed was a sound I could never replicate. A wet gurgling bubbled from below the blackness and the unmistakable sound of tearing meat. Silence fell as I moved closer, my toes just inches from the crumbling edge. There was movement in the darkness.

"*Meeeeat.*"

Without thinking, I returned to the kitchen and collected my own untouched meal. I didn't wait for the sounds to start this time.

While I avoided the backyard for the rest of the day and into the evening, the noises began to grow. As I laid in bed, the floor vibrated and grumbled like an empty stomach. It called to me, all night. It was then that I realised the soft churning of my own stomach and my quickening pulse wasn't fear anymore, it was excitement. It longed for me.

The following morning, I served Peter his breakfast with a spring in my step. The skillet with three extra sausages sizzled on high.

"Who are they for?" He asked with a mouth full of eggs.

"Me," I replied nonchalantly. "Just extra hungry today."

He lifted another forkful into his gaping mouth. "Well don't get fat," he replied with grease on his wide lips.

After handing him his packed lunch, he shrugged his work jacket on—despite the heat—and I kissed him goodbye.

The sausages hadn't fully crisped before I was stabbing a fork into them and opening the backdoor—the smell luring the neighbor's drooling dog to the gaps in the fence. Overnight the hole had grown a further two yards wide. The sausages fell into the darkness in one and the gargling groans began. This time, I sat down beside it on the dry ground, feeling the rumbling of the earth beneath my hands.

Days turned to weeks and bigger the hole grew. It spanned the length of our yard, uprooted shrubbery and cracked the cemented paving slabs on our patio. It warped and cracked the ground until I could barely leave the backdoor without careful footing. I overcooked, undercooked and even burned dinners to give Peter a reason to leave leftovers. All so I could feed the growing hole.

To my relief, Peter had no reason to visit the backyard. He left for work in the mornings and returned in the evenings where he spent the night glued to the television, drooling over whatever the next thing the federal government wanted to sell us was; he'd have bought kitty litter if instructed. He had the perfect man's life, as far as anyone else was concerned. Besides, I'd never been disobedient before so I'd never given him a reason for suspicion. Well, that was what I thought.

It was a Tuesday afternoon; I tended the yard. There I dropped overdone bacon and the slices of pre-sliced ham I'd told Peter were out of date. He came home on his lunchbreak butter with sandwiches in tow. Perhaps I had grown too comfortable for his liking. Began smiling to myself too much and humming in the kitchen while I cooked. Maybe Happy Wife Happy Life was just something people talked about, rather than practiced. He found me in the backyard after I'd failed to greet him at the door. I watched the confusion on his face pass like a wave, crashing into froths of malice as he took in the magnitude of the hole.

His words barely made a sound. "What have you done?"

There I stood, unable to form a sentence in response. The ground vibrated excitedly under my feet as he made his way towards me.

"You idiot!"

Then I heard it, softly calling out to me.

"*Meeeeat.*"

I glanced over to the center of the hole, where all the cracks met and formed the deepest part of the crevasse. Peter followed my gaze.

"What are you hiding?"

"Nothing." I protested but he changed course and headed straight for the large opening which used to be our yard. The voice grew in excitement as he got closer, emitting a shrill roar.

"*Meeeeat!*"

Peter pressed on with no indication of being swayed by the menacing voice. He looked back at me with his feet perched on the edge of the hole. Certain the blood had drained from my face, I stood still with my mouth agape.

"What?"

"Can't you hear it?"

"Hear what?"

I walked towards him with my hand outstretched to meet his. Peter was frightfully close to the crumbling edge. One false step and he would fall to certain death.

I swallowed hard and trod carefully. "Listen, how about some lunch?"

Peter scoffed. "No, I don't want any—"

"I wasn't talking to you."

THE NUNNERY

Nathan Perrin

You love coming to ancient places like this. It's what you're getting your doctorate in, after all. Catholic Monasticism. Contemplation, solitude. You love the silences that come along with mystic prayers and time spent reading. You're more than excited to go to a nunnery on a small island off the coast of Ireland, like the ones you read about as a little girl.

As the car pulls alongside the nunnery, you get out and are greeted by two Sisters.

"Hello, Sisters," you smile. "I'm Alyssa, with the university."

"Yes, of course, of course," says one of the Sisters. "Let's take your bags up to your room. I'm Sister Monica."

You smile again. You can't wait for the spiritual journey ahead of you.

The cab driver shoots you a grin, staring at you like you're a piece of meat as you take your bags out of the trunk.

"You single, miss?" he asks.

"Not interested," you say.

"Shame," he laughs.

You dismiss it, smile, and nod.

You sit in silence with the nuns eating dinner. Chicken with rice. Simple. You like the slow pace around here.

A Sister comes in with a shovel and bucket.

"Doing some gardening?" you ask.

She looks at you for a few seconds, smiles, and says, "Ah, yes. Just a bit of touchups around the island. Always needed."

You offer your hand, "I'm Alyssa."

"Sister James," the Sister shakes it back.

You wake up in the middle of the night to a faint monotone sound. It's coming from the sea.

As you open the blinds, you hear scuffling in the room next to you. You stare out and see the moon's reflection on the sea again. Same monotone sound.

In the distance, you think you hear screams - but they're too short and abrupt. You're not used to nature. You grew up in London and are used to busyness, noise. In the stillness and quiet, you are not sure what's normal and natural and what's not. Come to think of it, you're not sure if you can remember a single still moment in your life.

You look just below your window and notice the cemetery. It gives you chills, as if you shouldn't be seeing it. You close the blinds and try to sleep again.

You dream of your first night in an orphanage. It was also Catholic.

After watching your parents get shot in the street, all the fear and dread and shock hit you at once. You lie in bed and pray to God to take care of you because it seems no one else will.

You're sixteen years old and you begin to notice men staring at you constantly. You wear loose clothing but it doesn't stop them. You don't ever feel safe.

In the morning, Sister James walks back in with a shovel and dirt on her cassock.

"Mornin' Alyssa!" she says cheerfully.

"More work in the garden?" you ask.

"Aye, 'tis a beautiful mornin' for it."

"I would love to see you go through your daily routines and see what new things I notice."

"Aye, aye. The Lord's certainly grateful you're out here."

You turn on the voice recorder during the mass.

The priest makes eye contact with you, smiles, and keeps chanting in Latin.

You do the usual crosses and Catholic aerobics.

Sister Monica comes into the sanctuary. One passes you a note and sits down.

You open it up and read it.

Isaiah 34:2-3: "He will totally destroy them, he will give them over to slaughter. Their slain will be thrown out, their dead bodies will stink; the mountains will be soaked with their blood."

You try to remain objective as a researcher, not attached. You pretend there isn't any emotional value to the note that was passed to you hours ago. Yet, as you sit at dinner you can't help but notice that there is a tensity in the air.

"When was this convent established?" you ask.

"Mid-1500s," Sister James says. "Yes, 'twas a safe house for women on the run and all."

"The maids did good in helping them get here," Sister Monica nods.

"The maids?" you ask.

Silence.

"The maids, you know... they helped them cross the sea. All kinds of help. They were a group of women who made sure we were protected."

"Oh," you say. "Interesting."

In the distance, there is a scream.

You put down your fork and ask, "Did you hear that?"

"Aye," Sister James nods. "It's the wind is all. Nothin' to worry 'bout here."

"We hear that all the time," Sister Monica cuts into her steak.

You shake your head. This place is weird. In two days, you will leave and all be well. That's what you have to focus on.

"We did some readin' on you," Sister Monica smiles.

"What do you mean?" you ask.

"Grew up in an orphanage, dear," Sister James says. "I worked there. I remember you."

You try to fight back tears. The brief time at that orphanage felt like hell.

"Wanted to protect you, you know?" Sister James sips her tea. "Always prayed you would come our way. I'm an orphan too, you see"

"That's very nice," you force a smile. "I'm not interested in talking about it."

"You didn't feel led here?" Sister Monica asked.

You open your mouth to speak, and then remember the dream the night before.

"In a way," you say eventually.

You try to sleep that night but can't. The orphanage dream seems to be waiting to happen again.

The monotone noises in the distance continue.

Cursing out loud, you get up and put on your clothes. You have to figure out what's going on out there. At least it will distract you from the dread of the potential nightmare.

You slowly sneak out of your room and tiptoe out into the dark hallway.

The chilly night air smells salty, and you wish you'd worn your coat outside.

You hear the monotone noise again.

Walking towards it, you stumble over something and fall.

You get back up and look down.

The cab driver from two days ago is sprawled on the lawn, mouth open, blood dripping from his eyes.

They look like the eyes of your parents the night they were killed in front of you.

You scream.

The other nuns put a coat around you as you try to sip tea.
"We have to call the police," you say.
"We shall do no such thing," Sister James shakes her head.
"Why?"
"It would ruin the sanctity and pact of our island."
"What?"
"There's a spiritual world in the sea, Alyssa. They keep us safe here in our convent. That cab driver must've been up to no good for him to get killed like that."
You pause, "So... when you said maids earlier..."
"Mermaids," Sister Monica interrupted.
"You expect me to believe that?"

"We don't expect you to believe much. We're just Catholics over here recognizin' what we're seein'. We don't understand 'em, but they keep us safe and that's what matters."

"Safe from who?"

"You know who. The world. Cruel men. People who are up to no good. There's a whole spiritual world under the water. Nobody talks about it. Ghosts and demons and mermaids and the like. They don't like the way things are up here, so they take care of us."

"You don't have to worry about it," Sister James puts her hand on you. "In the mornin', we'll do a prayer and I'll show you around."

You can't believe this is happening. You won't believe it's happening.

Try to get some distance, you tell yourself. It's best to lay low until you get out. These nuns could be plotting to kill you too if you act up. Nope, best get out in one piece. The boat won't visit until tomorrow. Just keep it all inside.

"When you were in the orphanage," Sister James smiles, "didn't you wish that there was someone there to protect you? Well, we have that here. You don't have to worry about a thing."

You bite your tongue and nod your head.

When the sun rises, Sister James wakes you up and grabs your hand. You sleepily walk outside with a robe on. You see the driver laying in the grass again. His skin is gray, the blood has now dried on his face. You turn your face away.

"It's not your parents, love," Sister James grabs your hand. "Look and see. This is good."

Sister James guides your hand to the cab driver's forehead. It's cold, clammy.

You see him - no, you are him - last night.

He walks up to the shore after seeing a woman lying on the beach. He senses concern but there is that deep, dark thought inside you - a thought you've never had before. Violent, brief fantasies.

He smiles as he walks up to the girl, asks her if she's okay.

The woman stares back at him, he notices her eyes are glowing and her hair is covering her breasts. He looks down at her lower body and sees glimmering scales and two fins.

Suddenly she doesn't seem so entrancing.

She laughs at him and opens her mouth. Her eyes, my God, her eyes. He feels his soul being sucked out from his mouth and eyes. Struggling to scream he runs back up the hill towards the nunnery.

Yes, the nuns can help. Yes, yes, yes, ye-

He falls to the ground and watches the stars in the sky dim more and more.

The worst thing, like one of the unspeakable things he almost did to the creature on the beach, runs in front of his memory. He knows his soul somehow will be trapped with her forever. There's nothing he can do. He made his choice.

He accepts hell.

You back away screaming.

Sister James holds you while you weep.

The world isn't like this. It can't be this cruel.

"The souls of the wicked that come here stay in that ocean," says Sister James. "Those truly bound for there never leave. The maids keep us safe, don't you understand? The maids are there to protect us. The filthy degenerates that killed your parents? They would be there. You've got to accept this is the way it is."

You let out another sob.

You watch Sister James and Sister Monica dump the cab driver's body into a hole in the ground. They sprinkle holy water on him, say a few prayers. They then start shoveling dirt onto his body.

You are handed a shovel.

"We got to watch for one 'nother," Sister James pleads. "This is a rough world, miss."

You grab the shovel and start throwing dirt onto the cab driver's body, unable to forget either his death or the worst things he did.

With every flashback to the cab driver's misdeeds, you find yourself disgusted at how satisfied you suddenly feel that he's no longer in the world.

A few hours later, at dinner, soup is served.

You stare at it.

In the distance, more screams are heard. You bite your trembling lip.

You didn't even believe in hell before this. Now you have to believe in what you saw. There's no other sane explanation.

"More bread, Alyssa?" Sister Monica hands her a basket.

You nod your head as more screams echo throughout the island and valley.

You grab your bags and put them on the boat.

"Alyssa?" Sister James asks.

"Yes?" you say.

"You're always welcome back here," Sister James smiles. "Just don't judge us for what's kept us safe for centuries, missy. 'Member, they watch everything. They know."

You feel your heart drop.

Sister James hugs you, kisses you on the cheek.

"The way of things, I'm 'fraid," says Sister James. "'Truth be told I'm 'fraid that's the way it'll be 'til the good Lord comes back. Nothin' much we can do, you see."

You nod your head slowly and say, "I won't tell anyone."

"I know you won't," Sister James pats your arm. "If the world ever becomes too scary for you, know you have a place here waitin' for you."

You force a smile. You want to get off this island as fast as you can.

The ferry captain grabs your bags.

"Gotta go," you say quickly.

"I know you do," says Sister James. "Did you get what you wanted out of this?"

You shake your head, startled by your own honesty.

"Ah," Sister James chuckles. "Well, blessings on your journey as you try to find it out there."

She turns around and walks away.

You get on the ferry and let out quiet sobs of relief.

"You okay, miss?" asks the captain.

"Yes," you say. "Just get me out of here."

The ferry starts, and you see the island become smaller and smaller in the distance.

You hear the monotone noise again, this time above the sound of the engine.

You walk to the edge of the ferry and look down.

The water is clear as the souls of hundreds of thousands of dead are visible all at once, their mouths open and eyes terrified. The maids are torturing them, keeping them in chains. You see the cab driver. He makes one honest look at you, eyes asking you to help.

Your eyes drift to the right and you see the people who killed your parents also being tortured. It brings a sense of calm to your soul. Then something snaps you out of it - you gasp, turn around, and close your eyes.

After a few seconds, you peer over again and see nothing but blue green water.

You sit on the deck and look at the clouds in the sky briefly.

Nothing will ever be the same for you again.

But then you do some thinking.

Is it better to try to readjust to the world after what you've experienced and seen? Is it honestly the worst thing to have guaranteed safety? Is an ancient system of justice really worse than what you have in London? London is where your parents were killed. London is where you feel all alone. London is where nowhere feels safe.

You don't want to imagine trying to readjust. You don't want to think about how you'll be haunted for the rest of your days after what you've seen. The doctorate, the fake friends, the future you once dreamed doesn't make sense any more.

The harm done to you over the years by people who got away with it... what would happen if that hurt never happened to you again? You realize there is a greater possibility of happiness on the island than there is on the mainland. At least there, you will never get hurt. You will never have to take a risk again. There, you're not an orphan. There, you don't have to explain to friends and potential lovers why there's no one to take them home to.

You can sleep soundly at night knowing some... thing is watching over you. For the last fifteen years of your life, you couldn't say that you felt any sense of comfort in the night. But you could if you lived at the nunnery.

Can't say the same about London. Not by a long shot.

You get up and see the nunnery in the distance.

"No," you whisper.

You walk to the ferry captain, slip him the rest of the money from your purse, and ask him to take you back.

THE PRIESTS

Alexander Zelenyj

For the Son of Man came to seek and to save the lost.
- Luke 19:10

I: The House

Pastor Geoffrey Garfield was rinsing the pewter donation bowl behind the rectory when he saw the figure shambling in from the field. It used the narrow balding footpath that wound through the wild grass and the woods beyond, and which led to exactly where Garfield stood, brows knitted together as he squinted in the milky-aired dawn. Initially he'd thought it was a small group of men with arms wrapped about one another, perhaps friends, perhaps drunken revellers, though the town, with its main street of taverns and brothels, lay in the opposite direction from which they came.

Soon though, he understood that it was no group of men.

It moved in a peculiar manner, partly shuffling, partly swaying, and seemingly turning about full circle, time and again, as it came forward. At first Pastor Garfield thought it an ungainly method of locomotion, but the longer he watched, bewitched, he understood the fluidity and alien grace of its movement.

As the figure drew closer the Pastor's jaw dropped and the pewter bowl fell from his fingers to land with a flat wallop in the mud at his feet while he clutched the silver crucifix hanging about his neck through his vestments.

"I have heard of you," Pastor Garfield said. "The name they call you has traveled this land far and wide, though most—myself included—might not have believed the stories."

They were standing facing one another within the rectory. It was swathed in a patchwork of ill-fitting, dirty rags, their stench hanging in the warm air. It clutched a grimy satchel protectively in one of its hands. The Pastor stood with his back to the entrance to the church proper, where tapers cast an inviting glow in the expansive room.

"Yes, I seem to have become the stuff of urban legend or nightmare," said one of the voices of the figure before the Pastor.

And another of its voices said, "Though I believe the main of the tales you hear are not very accurate."

And the third of its voices said, "Which name do you refer to, Father? Horror? Monster? Sideshow attraction?"

Pastor Garfield said, "Men call you . . . the Priests."

"Ah yes," said all of its voices in unison, a strangely sibilant sound. "They call me that as well."

Indeed, its name had traveled by word of mouth over the years, and grown to become something like a dark tale by which mothers and fathers would coerce their wayward children to go to sleep—sleep, children, or the Priests will come for you in the wee hours, and take you far south of Heaven. The Priests was, though, no figment of the imagination but rather, as Garfield now saw, a real-life abnormality, a freak of nature, a strange being comprised of three bodies linked as one like a bizarre Siamese triplet. Each of its bodies was joined at the shoulders and faced inwards with its heads bowed eternally together, giving the name by which it was most known for its resemblance to a trio of men leaned together in earnest prayer, though many frowned upon such a sacrilegious moniker.

Pastor Garfield, still awed by the reality of the creature, sought to introduce as normal an atmosphere between them as he was able. Gesturing to the couch he said, "Please, sit." And then, "Can you . . . That is to say, are you able . . . to sit?" He felt foolish asking, felt that it was surely an imbecilic question, but then he had never met with such a scenario before.

"Yes," said one of the Priests' voices, though the Pastor couldn't tell which body had spoken. Its other voices echoed, "Thank you, Father." "Thank you."

He watched amazed as the creature drew itself upon the couch in a complex yet graceful movement of its peculiar body, folding its limbs queerly so that two of its bodies rested along the edge of the couch cushions, their combined weight holding aloft the third body, whose legs lay crossed on the cushion while its torso remained suspended in the open air beyond.

"Are you . . . comfortable?"

"Yes."

"Very much so."

"Thank you, Father."

Pastor Garfield seated himself across from the Priests, in the sister wood and plush armchair. Folding his hands across his lap, he looked at the creature levelly and said, "Where did you come from, my children? And what . . . what exactly are you, if I may be so bold?"

"I do not know," said the three voices of the Priests as one. "I only know that I am." One of its voices added, almost as an afterthought and with a hint of mild amusement, "You may refer to me in the singular, Pastor. For I am one person."

Another of its voices said, "One."

A third said, "Three-in-one."

"Oh, yes, I see," said Pastor Garfield. "I apologize. Please forgive me, my child. I've never met with someone quite like you before."

"No," said a voice of the Priests.

"You have not," said another.

"Three-in-one," said a third.

"Why . . . Why have you come here?" said Pastor Garfield.

The Priests paused and after some deliberation, during which the Pastor had the distinct feeling that the being wasn't so much considering its words but conferring among each of its individual bodies or minds, one of its voices said, "Why do I go anywhere?" and another voice answered, "I seek salvation," and another voice said, "If salvation is to be found in this world." And then together, in a manner that unsettled the Pastor, the three voices in unison said, "Perhaps fate brought me here. Perhaps one such as I, whom the world has given the name of the Priests, was destined from the beginning to conclude its journey in a place like this, an oasis in the heart of this world where oases are very few and far between."

A pained expression came over Pastor Garfield's face. "This world . . . You must know of its savagery," he said. "The world is a hard place for most men."

The Priests nodded its heads, and Garfield guessed the expressions it wore were creased with bitter remembrances. He'd initially wished to be able to see its individual faces, to look it in the eyes, but in that moment found himself relieved that he could not.

"A place of hardness," said one of its voices.

And another said, "And sadness."

And a third said, "And wickedness everywhere."

The Priests, weary from its long journey, sagged on the couch as if sleep were pulling it down, and yet the need to unburden itself of its long tale kept it awake. And so it talked and talked, and the things it spoke of seemed very foreign and unreal to the Pastor, yet rooted in a reality all-too believable given what he knew of humankind, so that it felt as though the Priests spoke from some strange midway point, some place between dream and reality. And oh, what a place it was. What a sad, aching country it was.

II: What the World Said

"One body belongs to an idiot—it cannot think! It drools and it gibbers and it jabbers!"

Individual voices rose above the crowd's general murmurings. "Let's see it!"

"Show us the monster, barker!"

"Freak! Freak!"

The carny, smiling triumphantly, stepped aside in perfect synchrony with his assistant, a gaunt pimple-faced twelve-year-old boy he'd trained well in his simpleton's tasks, who pulled heavily on a rope as stout as a grown man's forearm. The tattered brown curtain behind them lifted upwards from the wooden stage floor. Voices rose from the greater murmur of the crowd, throwing themselves toward the small wooden stage erected along one side of the stained tent. Smoke hung in a dense cloud over the heads of the people, billowing upwards into the domed curvature of the small tent's ceiling.

"Behold!" the carny shouted.

Gasps and shouts and whispers of disbelief and horror from the people, as the Priests lay revealed, standing naked underneath the plain light of the gas lamps mounted on either side of the tiny stage.

The carny struggled over the crowd-voice: "One of the beings has a great intellect and that, ladies and gentlemen, is a true tragedy for it is trapped between the idiot and . . . the other!"

The carny's wooden stick smacked one of the Priests' heads viciously. The crowd gasped, held spellbound by the dark origin of the being that spilled from the carny. He spat, "And this final body, oh! this final body is the truly horrifying one, for it hungers for human flesh and for the soft flesh of babies most especially! It feels only hunger and fury and lashes out in violence whenever opportunity arises! Beware, ladies and gentlemen!"

The shouts of the rowdy crowd grew more unruly still. They were eager to see proof of the spectacle of the horror, to decide whether it was grotesque enough for their satisfaction and worth the price of admission into the gloomy tent. The carny, his spiel timed to perfection after the many long months of touring the carnival circuit, roared, "Turn it around! Show the people the horrors!" And he and his young assistant slipped wooden sticks among the intertwined bodies of the Priests and pushed it and pushed it, turning the helpless being around in a circle for those gathered to see. It spun and it spun, its three pairs of bare, callused feet pattering along the wooden stage floor, its penises releasing the streams of urine that its bladders could no longer contain for the fear filling its pounding hearts.

Cries of horror and disgust rose on the smoky air. Fruit and stones and crumpled papers pelted the Priests as it cowered its three bodies closer together in a futile bid for preservation. Its voices whispered beseechingly all throughout the assault:

"It's not true—I am no monster."

"I am a man."

"I have good in my hearts."

But no one heard through the emphatic din.

III: What the Women Said

In the warm cave darkness a voice said, "I have the need."

"Yes, the need is strong," said a second voice.

The third said, "I'll have a tug."

"Three tugs. Three-in-one," said the second, getting to work by swivelling its left arm down and grasping the flaccid penis of the first, and vice versa, until each penis of the Priests was held by a hot hand. Three bodies; one gestalt, a single home of connected limbs: like any other person, it satisfied itself when it needed to.

The Priests' breathing grew louder in the cave. After a moment, the voices spoke together. "This is no good. I need more."

"Do I dare?" one of its voices ruminated.

"Yes," another said. "Yes."

Without further discussion the Priests slipped from its alcove set into the hillside along the edge of the woods where it had found shelter after fleeing the carnival, and made its way towards the lights of the town glowing like embers at the base of the hill in the hot summer night.

The toothless prostitute slipped between the Priests' web of arms and legs. Standing there in the midst of the three bodies, she looked claustrophobic. Fear and revulsion vied for control of her features, but her need for money won out and she smiled grimly.

"What's your boys' pleasure?" she said.

"I am but one," said the voice in her ear.

"Three-in-one," said the mouth beside her.

"One," said the head which she faced inside the meat-web. "Well, if you want it, you gotta pay for all three of you. That's about fair, I'd say."

After a moment of deliberation, the Priests said, "As you wish." In a life of abject poverty, the meagre hoard of coins it had stolen over the years was a treasure, and difficult to part with. But some needs had to be met no matter the cost.

"But know that I am, in fact, one."

"Three-in-one. Three-in-one."

The prostitute, with raised eyebrow, began unlacing herself and said, "Okay then. How would you like it, sir?"

The Priests passed her around between its three bodies. While one filled her from behind another would fondle her large swaying breasts, holding her in place, while the third stroked her thighs or ran fingers through her curls. Its faces' laboured breathing was loud and hot in the confined space.

When it was finished, the prostitute disengaged herself from the weird embrace of the Priests and stood beside it in the alley counting her money with hands that trembled, making the task difficult.

The voices of the Priests said:
"Thank you. You are a beautiful woman."
"Beautiful."
"Thank you for being with me, one with three-in-one."

She watched the being as it moved deeper into the alley darkness in its strange shuffling-spinning manner like a wheel made of interlocked men. The Priests watched the prostitute too, for as it moved it spun about, giving each of its pairs of eyes the opportunity to see the woman standing in the fringe of streetlight glow that invaded the narrow alley. The Priests could tell by the expression on her face that the memory of the thick and otherworldly embrace she'd experienced would haunt her, though something else in her eyes betrayed some deeper troubling thought. Perhaps no one in all her years of such clandestine meetings had ever called her beautiful.

IV: What Science Said

"Okay, let's have a listen."

The Priests briefly came into the care—though the Priests would have called it possession—of a physician. Dr. Walter Stokes had discovered the Priests as part of a traveling sideshow and purchased its freedom from the show's proprietor. Immediately upon securing the Priests, he'd brought it to his office under cover of nightfall for an examination.

Reaching a trembling hand inside the space made by the Priests' connected bodies, he moved his stethoscope with great—if unsteady—deliberation from one of its chests to the next to the next. As his hand moved the little silver device, his mouth moved as if of its own volition, murmuring words like, "Incredible", "Amazing", "Miraculous", and culminating with, "Sweet Lord, can this be, can this really be?"

After a moment Stokes straightened and, staring with wide eyes, said, "Have you but one personality, or three?"

"I have three, each of which is distinct from the others, though we each want the same things. We do not squabble, we do not argue, for we agree on all things."

"But you experience those things . . . individually?"

"In a manner of speaking, yes," said the three voices of the Priests as one, "Though as you can see from the way which I answer your questions—as one—I am of one mind. My personalities give comfort to one another, and strength, but they all inform and speak of one mind. Somehow I am, and have always been . . . three together as one."

"As with any other person in the world, many different moods and characteristics make up who I am," added another voice of the Priests.

The physician stared at the Priests raptly. "Amazing," he said again. "I'm finding it difficult to understand, but I am fascinated beyond words." Then, fiddling with the stethoscope, moving it along one of the Priests' backs, he said, "Have you heard of Joseph Merrick? The so-called Elephant Man?"

"Yes," said one of the voices of the Priests, while the other voices murmured agreement too. Then a second voice from within the circle of the being said, "I feel sorrow for Mr. Merrick. Great sorrow."

"Yes, great sorrow."

"My hearts go out to him."

A curious and rather indignant expression seeped its way into Dr. Stokes' features. He said, "And why do you feel sorrow for Mr. Merrick, who has shown such courage in the face of his condition, and such an un-guessed and admirable predilection for the arts?"

"Because he is alone," said a voice from inside the circle of the Priests, silencing the doctor.

"Yes, alone."

"One. Only one."

The night outside the physician's office window had grown quiet. The moon seemed frozen in its sky of pitch, never to crawl into the west again.

"Will you let me study you?" said Dr. Stokes.

"Yes," answered the Priests as one, disliking the lie it so easily gave the doctor, knowing of course that it could do nothing else if it were to survive, for it had seen the look in the man's eyes: a cold and calculating avarice the likes of which it had seen plenty of in its years among men. By morning it had slipped away undetected from the cheap motel room the doctor had rented for it, no doubt leaving its short-lived personal physician wondering whether the madness of his previous evening's appointment had actually transpired at all, whether something like it had any place in the bright day-lighted world he knew, where nightmares didn't really exist among his usual patients with their everyday sicknesses and complaints.

It was hours after making its escape under cover of a sudden and violent rainstorm, while the Priests was taking a rest from its trek through the sodden, thundering night, that it crossed paths with a drunk man stumbling toward his bed somewhere. The man stopped short, squinting through the rain and shadows at the strange form hunkered down alongside the wall of the squat building in the alley, cocking an ear at the sound of its voices.

"Who's that?" he called, and then, more belligerently, "What the hell are you whispering over there?"

"A prayer, friend," said one of its voices.

The man staggered closer. In the brief illumination thrown from a flash of lightning he saw the Priests in all its strangeness. A gasp escaped him, and he hissed, "What demon prays during a storm like this?" The man's eyes were wide with horror. His hand went instinctively to his hip, where a knife was undoubtedly hidden beneath his shirt.

"Perhaps we pray for all of us."
"You and I, and everyone."
"All."

The man's expression of fear turned to one of disgust, and though he opened his mouth to speak no words came for he knew not what to say. Confusion came over him, which angered him, and so he only spat at the Priests and said, "Go to Hell, you fuckin' ugly demon! God save us from you!"

And the man stumbled on his way, careening from the rough brick walls of the buildings he passed, casting fearful glances behind him as he went.

The Priests remained where it was, making no effort to find shelter from the storm. It stood very still in the deluge, in the centre of the widening pool of muddy water in the centre of the alley, as if waiting for a word or sign from the tumultuous sky, or perhaps waiting to feel cleansed.

V: What the Children Said

"Has anyone ever loved you?" said the little blonde-haired girl, eyes wide and probing.

The Priests looked down on the child from its place inside the observation tank on the small wooden stage. Through the scratched face of the thin protective glass the girl was queerly elongated, making her face mean and severe, unless of course this was the beginnings in her face of the future woman peering through. The Priests' answer fell quickly and sure in the stuffy air of the display case, rising into the heights of the barn beyond, in which the observation tank had been erected in this small town whose name it would never learn but whose people seemed so much like those of all the other nameless small towns through which the carnival show passed.

"I have myself."

"Three-in-one."

"One."

The little girl considered this for a moment. Then she said, "You're so ugly I think no one ever loved you or ever will."

And she turned quickly on her heel and marched the length of the barn and out its open doors, to where her parents waited for her. Their laughter reached the Priests inside its tank, sounding muted and nervous but no less vindictive.

In a single hushed voice the Priests called after the girl, "I'm sorry for you, child. But it is you, beneath your pretty cherub's face, that is truly and deeply ugly."

VI: What the Family Said

But there was goodness in the world, too, the Priests learned. Rare people, like Reginald Bonnycott Bendum, ringmaster of a traveling circus and father to its menagerie of strange men and women and children and beasts. The Priests had approached Bendum when the freak show it was a part of crossed paths with his own, much larger traveling spectacle. The Priests, expecting much the same reaction from him as it received from most people, was surprised at the man's warmth and the friendship he offered without any hint of avarice or dishonesty.

"When you join my traveling show," he'd proclaimed with a great smile on his lips and the twinkle in his eye for which he was known far and wide, "You become a part of my family."

The days that followed were good ones. The Priests made friends, shared sympathetic stories with troupe members, felt acceptance for the first time in its life. But over the months, something grew inside the hearts of the Priests, which it took quite some time for it to recognize as a great unrest, and a great need for knowledge that its newfound life—as wondrous and good as it was—could not satisfy.

One evening the ringmaster welcomed the Priests into the study of his lavish trailer following its appearance in the freak tent several hours earlier. He left the room and returned a moment later with refreshments for himself and his guest, and stopped short in the doorway. Peering between the Priests' connected network of limbs he saw that it had retrieved a book from one of the shelves which lined the room. It was holding the volume between its heads and, cocking an ear, the ringmaster discerned its voices taking turns speaking softly, one after another after another.

"'I opened my eyes upon a strange and weird landscape.'"

"'I knew that I was on Mars.'"

"'Not once did I question either my sanity or my wakefulness.'"

Into the silence following the Priests' voices, Reginald Bonnycott Bendum said, "My Lord, you're able to read!"

The Priests quickly lowered the book in its hands. "Forgive me, sir. I hope I have not been rude and too liberal in reading from one of your books."

Another of its voices, equally flustered, said, "Your shelves hold so many volumes, it was hard to resist investigating them further."

"So many books," said its third voice. "So many voices." Indeed, the ringmaster was an avid reader, and loved strange and wondrous tales best of all. He'd been a collector of books for many years, and his travels to different cities afforded him the luxury of visiting many different bookshops.

"Of course you haven't been rude at all, my friend," Bendum said. "Please feel free. I just . . . I'm only a little surprised that you're able to read, though I suppose I shouldn't be—your eloquence should have told me."

"Books have been a solace and escape for me often throughout the years," the Priests said, "Though I have not been able to read nearly as much as I would have liked, for books are difficult to come by."

Another of its voices said, "I no longer recall how or when I learned to read."

And a third voice finished, "But I've been grateful for the gift as long as I can remember."

"You'll find no better escape than that which you hold in your hands now," the ringmaster said. "Mr. Burroughs is a master of taking his reader away, whether into time-lost jungles or places beyond the stars."

"Yes, I can see that," said the Priests.

"I feel the refuge in these pages," said the Priests.

"Refuge," said the Priests. "Haven."

"The book is yours," said the ringmaster.

The Priests sucked in its breaths as one. "But sir! I cannot accept such a generous gift . . ."

"You can, and you will," said Bendum with conviction, a glimmer in his eyes. "Please, my friend. Consider it . . . a farewell gift, from one friend to another."

"Then you know that I seek answers that your nomad caravan cannot give me," said a voice of the Priests wondrously, sadly.

"I thought as much, my friend," conceded Bendum. "I had a feeling that's what you wanted to speak to me about this evening." Then, "Who raised you, when you were a child? Have you no ties to this person or persons today?"

"I do not know," said a voice of the Priests.

"I no longer recall—it was so long ago," said another.

A third voice said, "I remember a woman—a very old woman—but the memory of her is seen as if through a fog. I do not know who she was, but have always known in my hearts that she was not my true mother."

"I have always believed," said another voice, "That bringing me into the world was her final act, for she surely must have died during what was certainly a very difficult childbirth."

A grim chuckling came from the Priests at this, conjuring horrifying visions in the old man's eyes, though he couldn't help but chuckle himself at the being's dark humour. Bendum nodded. "If I may ask, then what do you remember from your early life? As a child? Of the people whom tended you?"

"My earliest memories," said the Priests, "are pain-filled."

"Cages and strangers all the time."

"Men staring, disgusted, women horrified."

"Some images are only half-formed, it seems."

"For I may have buried them."

"Deeply. In deep, deep places."

"For bad memories are best to be interred as deeply as possible."

The old ringmaster thought of his travelling circus, and the countless visitors to their show who came to gawk at the spectacle of them all in their collective strangeness. They survived as any family should, through the simple solidarity of standing up for one another, always. Strength in numbers and familiarity and love, so that at times it even seemed to be the case that the outside world, and not the strange, closed-off internal world of the traveling show, housed the true freaks and horrors.

"I wish you would stay. You have a family here anytime you want it," said Bendum. He was thinking of his beloved menagerie of misfits: the dog boy; the mermaid; the monkey-boy; the octopus baby; the bearded woman; the clowns and geeks and acrobats and sword-swallowers and masked ballyhoo players. And this unique being before him now, a person like no other, but for its hearts, which were good hearts like those of his other troupe members.

"I have a family here," said the three voices of the Priests as one.

"Three-in-one," said one of its voices.

"Three-in-one," echoed another.

And together, "I seek greater answers, from a greater source, about this world in which I live, and about other worlds elsewhere."

The ringmaster stared with wonder at the Priests. A great respect for the being filled him. "My friend. My dear, dear friend," he said. "You are a beautiful creature. And a miracle among us all. I'm so grateful for—I'm so honoured by—the time you've spent with us." And he wept.

The ringmaster and the Priests cried together in the murky trailer, while the world outside marched on.

VI: The Kingdom

Into the warm air of the rectory, one of the Priests' voices said, "There is so much more I have not even begun to tell, Pastor Garfield. So much more, in the years following my self-exile from my circus family . . .

"Once, years ago, a gang of drunk men found me seeking solace in a little-frequented alley in a town whose name I can no longer remember." Two of its voices fell silent, and a third voice continued its tale, "These men were horrified at the thing they discovered seeking shelter amid the refuse and rat-nests, but hid their horror behind their anger and false bravado." And another of its voices finished the dark tale: "These men took turns raping each of my bodies, three men at a time. Their dark game went on and on."

Another of its voices said, "One of the men broke a bottle across the back of this head." The Pastor watched in mute horror as one of the Priests' heads waggled slowly from side to side. Indeed, a long and thick, time-faded lump scarred the head from crown to nearly the base of the neck.

A different voice said, "And once, long ago, came a time I sought salvation in a place of monastic peace."

"Yes," it said with another of its mouths, and it was all it said, as if the subject was too difficult to continue, until its third voice said, "But even the good monks of the monastery barred my way at their gates, believing I to be an aberration of another world that would seek to harm them in their stronghold of peace."

"Perhaps they were merely frightened," it said, "for maybe they saw me as a strange and gruesome broken reflection of themselves?"

"Yes, perhaps," mused its third voice with what sounded like embittered amusement.

A cynical laugh escaped one of the Priests' mouths, though the Pastor knew not which. Garfield felt a great weight in his chest. As a rule, he sought to understand and be compassionate to his fellow man; but when man proved time and again the unending reserves of his barbarism, it was a Herculean task, and one that the Pastor found more and more difficult to achieve.

"I'm . . . I'm so very sorry for the things you have suffered," he said, knowing of course how paltry the words were.

One of the Priests' voices said, "Many times have children screamed in horror." Another voice, "And ran away screaming still." Another voice: "Or pelted me with stones, and spit on me and cursed me." But the first voice amended, "But they are children, and children, being pure beings, only become sullied by what they learn from those around them. They are to blame, the teachers of children, never the children themselves."

After a moment's pause one of its voices said, "But there are some who are good. The ringmaster, Reginald Bonnycott Bendum, for one."

"Yes," said Pastor Garfield. "He sounds like a good and honourable soul."

"Yes," the Priests said together. "A rare soul indeed."

Garfield fretted, knotting his fingers behind his back. "I wish I could do something. But I wonder, if a good soul like your ringmaster friend was not able to give you what you seek, in a place of care and understanding, then . . . what can I do for you, my children? My child? What am I able to do for you? Why have you sought me out?" He felt fear envelop him, as though the task was a challenge set before him by the Lord, but what if he hadn't the strength to complete it?

A voice of the Priests said, "I need to know whether my belief all these long years has been a foolish one. Whether what my hearts have always told me is wrong."

Another of the Priests' voices said, "Is there a place?"

"A place?" said Garfield.

The voices said:

"A place of salvation."

"A place of sanctuary and refuge."

"Is there Paradise? Does the fortress of Heaven truly exist beyond this world that is burning away in the great fire of its own making?"

Pastor Garfield considered the weight of the things he'd been told by the creature; and he considered what he knew of the world's dark history; and of the few good-hearted people to whom he preached each day and whom he considered true friends. And he answered honestly.

"Yes. There is such a place. There has to be, or else why would any of us be here at all?"

The Priests said, in a single sibilant and imploring voice: "Show me."

Pastor Garfield nodded. Something flared into life inside him. His mission lay revealed. He'd received the Call long ago when he'd still been a young man, but this, this was a renewal of his true purpose. He opened his mouth to speak but the Priests stopped him.

"But first, Father, I must confess, for I have sinned."

Pastor Garfield listened to the Priests' tale, of a dark winter's night in a small nameless town; a tale of another hard-hearted man—a tavern-keeper, angered by the vagrant he'd found sheltering from the cold within the alcove of his establishment's rear doorway; horrified by what he found when he'd kicked this sleeping bum awake, sending the strange creature stumbling out into the alley where the moonlight revealed it in all its gruesomeness. This man had followed the Priests as it fled down the alley as if intoxicated with the vision of it, unable to leave it be, hounding it with the terrible things he called it, growing angrier and bolder in his bullying until, finally, he committed the crime no other had ever done to the Priests-- he squeezed himself through the tangled, interconnected web of the Priests' fused limbs and taken up vile residence in their midst so that he could look into each of its faces, and he spit scornfully into each of these faces of shame. Helpless, unable to escape with the invading man tangled inside of its limbs, the

Priests did what it had to. For it was this final violation of its private self, the only space it had ever had to itself as a shield from the prying eyes of the world, that proved too much for the Priests to bear, and it acted on its humanity—proving that it indeed had the hearts of men—and it held the man tightly in its three-bodied, unyielding embrace, and used the teeth of its three mouths to tear the man's throat out. Three-in-one, strong in the throes of the pain filling its hearts, against one weak and heartless man.

In the wake of its story, the Priests stood silently, shuddering with the weight of the words it had finally spoken aloud to another man after years of silence.

And Pastor Garfield, his jaw trembling and his eyes hard and inscrutable, said, "No, my son. You've committed no sin at all. For some men are Lucifer Himself, risen up from the molten pit to which he was banished, to spread the fire of His burning heart in this beautiful but harsh world."

The weeping that then poured from the Priests undid Pastor Garfield, for it was a joyful weeping the likes of which he'd never before heard in his long years of preaching the good Word; and he wept, too.

Later that night, something awakened Pastor Garfield from the dark dream he dreamed—a dream of fire and darkness engulfing him—and he sat up in bed, sweating a cold sweat and listening to the wind whispering in the eaves. Then, beyond its insistent voice, he discerned another sound. Listening hard, he slipped from the bed and donning his robe drifted across the room and into the hall outside. He followed the sound, coming to the rectory doorway and facing the church beyond. There, lit in a halo of warm orange light thrown from the sputtering candles in the candelabra, he found the Priests kneeling on the wooden floor, heads bowed together as ever. Its synchronized whispered voices came to him: the recitation of the Lord's prayer comforted him, warmed him in the chill air.

Garfield listened to the Priests' prayer, its physical deformity and its place before the altar imbuing it with the appearance of a secret cabal conducting some clandestine rite. And he reprimanded himself for his wrongful judgment and fear when he'd first met this creature, and smiled in acceptance of what it truly was he saw convened within this house of the Lord he humbly tended: beauty, in all of its awesome and unexpected splendour.

And he went in silence to a place beside the Priests, and he knelt there too and added his voice to the prayer filling the room.

They turned at the knock on the heavy oak door, and the echoes it sent reverberating into the church's lofty reaches.

"Father," called a woman's voice from the other side of the door.

A note of hysteria edged the voice.

"My child," Pastor Garfield whispered to the Priests, eyes full with agitation.

"I understand," said the Priests as one. "I don't want to alarm this visitor with my unexpected presence and . . . strangeness." And it rose smoothly from the floor, making quickly for the shadows of the rectory to one side of the altar.

Pastor Garfield raised a hand, said, "Thank you, my child. If you could please wait within the rectory, only until I see what the trouble is." He hurried through the aisle formed by the pews to the door, pushed it wide to find Beatrice Salisbury shuddering in the wind, a blanket-wrapped bundle in her arms.

"Beatrice," he greeted her, smiling and stepping aside for her to enter the church.

"Hello Father," she said. "I'm sorry to have disturbed you at such an hour."

"Not at all, my child, not at all," he said. "How may I help you?" Her distraught expression chilled him. She held aloft the bundle and with one hand drew back a veil of blanket to reveal the child within. The soft skin of his face and neck was splotched with angry red spots. His eyes were puffy and mired shut with the same deep crimson marking.

"I'm scared for James, Father," she said. "He's been like this for days. Dr. Samuels examined him, and what he first took to be measles . . . well, it's proven to be something else. He doesn't know what to make of it. He said he's never seen nothing like it in all his years of medicine. And earlier this evening, James' cough worsened and . . . I found blood on his blanket."

She broke off, weeping, shoulders shuddering.

The Pastor placed a hand across the child's forehead, took it away quickly. "He's burning up!" he breathed.

"His fever broke a day or so ago, but came back last night worse than ever." Her eyes pleaded. "Father, I don't know what to do. Thomas thinks it's a curse, and the doctor couldn't help him so I thought maybe you could offer . . . a good word, or prayer?"

"Of course, my dear." Pastor Garfield took the child from its mother. With great care he parted its blankets to reveal his features more clearly. The child's face, he saw, was swollen and inflamed, and a dark black bruising had begun along the periphery of the red markings, calling to his mind cases of bubonic plague he'd seen photographs of in books. He knew not what the child's affliction was, but knew in his heart that it was deadly.

Beatrice turned at the soft sound behind them, and saw the Priests standing within the shadows of the vestibule leading into the rectory. She stared with wide eyes a moment before a scream tore from her, its echoes rebounding throughout the vaulted chamber. She drew back a step, faltered, and fainted, crashing to the floor before Pastor Garfield who, with the infant cradled in his arms, was unable to catch her.

"I'm sorry, Father!" said the Priests as one. "But I heard what the woman said, and wanted to console her."

"I wasn't thinking, Father," cried another of its voices.

"I'm so sorry," it said again. "I should have known what seeing me would do to her."

"Hush, my friend," Pastor Garfield said. "And wait here a moment." The baby wheezed thickly as he placed it gently onto the floor, lost inside the voluminous folds of its blankets. He then turned to administer to Beatrice, pulling her to a sitting posture leaning against the nearby pew. He went to retrieve some water and a towel from the interconnecting washroom, and as he returned into the main chamber, saw.

The Priests shuffled and spun with its peculiar grace to a place before the infant, and then carefully and with great deliberation stepped a pair of its legs over the baby so that the child lay directly in the midst of its three bodies. In this way the Priests was able to see the child clearly with each of its three pairs of eyes looking down upon it in its centre.

Garfield stood with towel and water in hand, and listened to its hushed voices carry across the echoing chamber.

"A beautiful child!"

"Oh, sweet baby boy, look at your golden curls!"

"A miracle! Just look at him!"

"Hush, little one, and save your strength."

"Yes, be quiet, child, and rest yourself."

"Hush, and soon your fever will go away."

"Hush, child, and sleep to awaken another morning—the world will be yours, some day."

"Yes, you have so much ahead of you."

"A long path."

"A long and good path."

"Sleep, and dream good dreams."

"You are not alone—you will have love in your life."

"Great and infinite love."

"The angels, they sing of you, and for you."

"Sleep, child."

"Sleep, and be well."

"Sleep."

As the Priests fell into silence so too did the child, his soft burbles eventually turning into the steady rhythmic breathing of deep sleep. The Priests continued to stand over the baby, its voices whispering a soothing melody, and though what it said the Pastor couldn't make out, the sound itself was a gentle, a nurturing, a peaceful sound, the rhythm and sound of impassioned prayer. And within the protective house of the Priests' tangle of limbs the child slept on, undisturbed.

Baby James' fever broke by the following morning. By the evening of that day the red spots on his face and neck and arms were subsiding, and no fever burned his brow. He slept fitfully at first, but then long and well, to awaken in the early evening with a mighty appetite and a healthy voice crying for his mother's breast. The child also spoke his first word that night, looking up into his mother's face and smiling: "Good," he'd said, and it had made both his mother and the Pastor cry. And then James slept again, burbling drowsily as he dreamed and dreamed his way towards the next day, and a long and healthy life.

To the child's mother Pastor Garfield explained that what she'd seen the night before was no abomination as she'd believed. He assured her that it was but a poor soul, with a good heart. And he explained what he'd witnessed himself, and given that baby James had recuperated so quickly in the aftermath of it, well . . . He left that up to Beatrice to decide for herself. Watching her weep with thanks told him her answer, and for this one step for all mankind in a better direction he was pleased. He implored her to make no mention of what she'd seen to anyone, to allow him the task of introducing his newfound companion to the townspeople at large; and though Beatrice had nodded in agreement, he doubted she would be able to resist telling her husband, Thomas, of what she'd seen, who would no doubt see witchcraft and curses at work, and in turn would spread this untruth among those who would listen.

But Garfield could only thank her for her understanding, hoping in his heart that she truly did believe and understand what he'd tried to explain to her, and watch her leave the church and head home with her recuperating child bundled in blankets against the chill November air.

It was later on in the morning when the Pastor opened the door to the small storage room he'd made up for the Priests the evening before. He found the creature sleeping, positioned in the same queer posture he'd seen it sitting in once before already; one of its bodies forming the base upon which its second body leaned partway, with the third body sitting upright, leaned back as far as it was able and in this way pulling against the weight of its companion bodies and serving to prop itself up. The Pastor stared in renewed wonder at the tangle of limbs, trying but failing to comprehend how this creature could have survived in the world for as long as it had, shuddering at the things it must have suffered through.

He noticed the book then, resting on the mattress among the protective shelter of the Priests' limbs; the light from the ajar door helped him see its tattered cover, and the faded picture adorning it, of a man and woman standing together on a barren and alien landscape, with a star-stippled sky reeling over them. By the light he read its title and author's name—A Princess of Mars by Edgar Rice Burroughs—and a smile creased his face. This then, was the Priests' Bible, its long-standing book of refuge and salvation. In that moment, Pastor Garfield understood truly the power of words and the gift of escape they could give those in need.

He remained there a while, tears on his cheeks, the sound of the Priests' three breathings soothing him where he stood watching from the doorway.

"I hope your dreams are good dreams," he said.

At this one of its heads, belonging to the body sitting semi-upright, stirred. Straining to see behind itself caused the other heads to stir too.

"I'm sorry," said Pastor Garfield, wiping at his eyes. "I know you must be tired. I just came to check on you, is all."

One of the Priest's voices, muddy with sleep, said, "No. Thank you for waking me, Pastor."

Another of its voices said, "I haven't slept this well in a long time. It must be nearly dawn. I feel refreshed."

The third of its voices said, "Thank you for allowing me lodgings here."

"It's nothing," Pastor Garfield said, waving his hands on the air. "I was washing up in the washroom down the hall, but am finished now. Feel free to use it if you wish to clean up before breakfast. You can find me in the rectory whenever you're ready."

"Thank you, Father," said the Priests as one.

They were seated at the small round oak dining table in the rectory's kitchen. The silence of the church proper beyond the door was a deep and heavy one. They'd spent the day reading, immersed in scripture, and felt rejuvenated, though their eyes were red and sore from strain.

"I've slept little and have thought long and hard, and I have two things to say to you, my child," said Pastor Garfield.

The Priests waited, silent and still.

"Firstly, whether or not what I saw and what transpired here last night was miraculous, as I do believe it was, it did tell me one thing: that you are a child of Heaven, and that He has seen fit that you walk upon His earth. You are loved. You have good in your hearts, and you are loved."

He paused a moment, emotion seizing him and making words difficult. Then he went on.

"And secondly: you may stay here if you wish. You have a place here with me, in this House, to work and study and to continue to do good while we wait together for the better place after the world we've known here, with its slow thinking and sadness and savagery."

"But Father," said a voice of the Priests, saying what was in the Pastor's heart: "What if others see me, and do not understand?"

"Yes," said another of its voices, "What if men come here, as they surely will now that my presence is known, and see and see only horror?"

"What if they come back with noose and torch and rifle?" said its third voice. "To vanquish the evil thing that they see, and the good man who fell under its spell and saw good in its hearts? Once the woman tells them of me, this thing may very well come to pass, as it came to pass so many times before, causing me to flee and seek refuge elsewhere only to learn, time and again, there was no refuge to be found, anywhere, but for perhaps the haven of a touring freak show traveling the dark lands."

"If only I too could fall asleep and wake up on Mars," said its voices together, and the Pastor saw that the Priests was cradling its treasured Burroughs book to itself.

Pastor Garfield nodded solemnly. When he spoke, his voice was hard as iron. "Let the people come. This House is a new and better House today than it was before. Let them come." And it was all he said.

He saw the shuddering of the Priests' shoulders, and knew that it was crying. He waited a moment, cleared his throat, and said, "One other thing . . . I've been thinking . . . You have been called many things in your life, and yet you've never owned a true name. I think it only appropriate that you have a name, for no good man should go without. You are a special and unique person, and after witnessing last night's miracle it seems to me that perhaps you represent a step forward, in a new and better direction for us all. And so I propose we call you . . . Adam."

He could foresee how his superiors in the church would react to such a choice; but then he knew how right it felt in his heart, and this was a voice with which he could not argue.

And although Pastor Garfield couldn't see the faces of the Priests as it sat huddled before him with its heads bowed towards each other, he was certain there was a great joy—like a miracle, like the light of true Paradise itself breaking through barriers of cloud to touch down on Earth—pouring forth from its three pairs of weeping eyes.

Father Garfield said grace and they ate their simple but good dinner in a silence punctuated only by the caterwauling of the wind through the high eaves of the church outside the rectory.

It wasn't long before the murmur of voices and movement carried through the night, the crunching of many feet through the autumn leaves littering the road leading to the church's steps. Pastor Garfield and the Priests looked up from the book they were reading together and made their way to stand at the threshold of the rectory's doorway, and looked out across the pews of the church. The flicker of torches and the shadows of those who wielded them played a violent dance on the stained-glass windows, casting gruesome demonic shadows crawling and leaping like blasphemy inside the immense room, across its walls and altar. The great murmuring voice of the crowd sounded much like the voices of the many crowds that had come to witness the Priests in the past, though perhaps louder now, and somehow angrier.

The Priests said, "Thank you, Father, for your kindness."

And, "Thank you for listening to my story."

And, "Thank you for sharing your House with me."

"Thank you," said Pastor Garfield, "For sharing your story with me. Now be strong, and trust in the strength and goodness of this House."

Adam, in a single voice, said, "Then let us pray together now, and wait for His answer."

The two men, side by side, recited the strongest words of salvation they knew in the darkening church, their four voices striving to be heard over the growing din of the people gathering outside the walls.

THICKER THAN WATER

Dylan T. Bosworth

I should have died when I was two. The memory of that day burrows through my head like a glistening centipede – its hundred legs painfully stabbing along the contours of my fleshy brain. Like a pile of maggots, reveling in their den of rot. That day consumes all other thoughts until there is nothing left. A squirming, festering mass of pain, mired in decay.

People tell me they're glad I survived when I get around to admitting I shouldn't be here, which is sort of rare, I suppose. I try not to think about it. Try not to remember what she did to me. To us.

Glad.

My mouth fills with venom every time I hear the word, and if I could just grab these people by the face and somehow jam my memories into them, stuff them into every orifice I can find until the blackness fills them as it fills me, eating away at their insides, razor wire shredding cords of flesh off the memories of their souls.

If people knew what I'd been left with, they wouldn't tell me they were glad for me. I often wondered growing up what outcome was worse – dying so young or living with surviving. But now I know. Without a doubt, I know.

My mother just died in prison, though, so there's that. I could talk about that all day. Over the years, I'd grown not to hate her, but I can't say that I was sorry to hear she was gone. I never knew the lady, to be honest, but I had a whole life behind me, spent avoiding pools and lakes, and especially rivers, and all I had to show for it was this stupid trauma. That's all she ever gave me.

I'm not sure what's worse there either. A life of trauma, or a life in prison? We'd both given each other something. What's the opposite of a gift?

It was her actions that got me here, and I guess her own actions that put her there, too; although the case could be made that it was my testimony that put her away upstate. It didn't matter anymore, though. She was gone and her sentence was over. Mine was far from it.

I was aborted, post-term by two years, and I crawled my way out of that river womb into a lifetime of torture.

Like I said, I don't like to talk about it, but if you're here to listen, allow me to sing you a song.

One morning after breakfast, my mother packed up my big brother and me (I say *big*, but, Christ, he was only three). She drove us to this little lot that had been cleared out next to the river – a place where people launched their kayaks and canoes. We sat by the edge of the river and watched the ducks land and groom themselves until the sky darkened to that surreal sort of pink that sometimes happens after long, happy days in the sun that you want to never end.

Before we left, my mom had my brother and me wandering around the clearing on a mission to find the biggest rocks we could. I had an impressive collection of big round ones for which I needed two hands that were starting to pile up around my mother's feet, and my big brother had two halves of a cinder block he could barely carry without dropping in the dirt.

Anyway, she pulled two bookbags out of the car, and my brother and I were so excited because we hadn't even seen the inside of a school yet, and I guess that those bags got us thinking that that's where we were headed for some reason. Even when my mom was taking all our rocks and stuffing them into the little bags, and then tying our bags together, all I remember feeling even then was excitement. Even as she took the excess strap that hung off the back of the tightening clasps and tied the bags bear-hug tight around our bellies, my two-year-old brain was still all sorts of amped up. Bright eyed and full of motion, ready to face something new.

She walked out into the water with us, both of us kids held high up by her shoulders until we were as deep as my mother's neck. I can't imagine it was easy for her, us being weighed down with all those rocks in our bags, either, but as she waddled out to where she felt was good enough, she just let us fall from her arms. I've often wondered what was harder for her. Carrying us out there, or letting us go.

So yeah, I was aborted. Twenty-six months, three days, post-term. That river birthed me back onto the bank sometime later, and now I had a newer, grander mother – no matter how afraid of her ripples and waves I'd be for the next twenty-six years. She was kinder than my real mother, in a way. I just wished she'd have given me my brother back at the time.

I said I'd grown not to hate her, my mom, and that's true, but it wasn't time and introspection that had healed those wounds. Shoot, I think I understood in the only way a toddler could at the time that it wasn't her fault at all.

But the old lady who'd gone fishing with her husband who found me washed up on the bank, all tangled in briars and overhang, she saw my mom still sitting there on the edge of the river, staring at where she'd dumped us to drown. When the police came, it was night, and I watched my mom get rolled away in the back of a police car while I sat on the edge of an opened ambulance, wrapped tightly in a blanket that made me feel like spiders were crawling all over my bare skin..

No divers or skimmers or whatever you call the people that drag the lake had found my brother's body, and I knew they never would. I'd seen what took him down there in the deep of the river. The crevasse that opened with its pale blue light, and the clawed hands that reached up like flowing seaweed to grab at us as we floated down, down to the bed of the river. All those lilting voices, like I'd imagined angels must sound, singing to us as the claws shredded my big brother, and inadvertently cut loose the ties that bound me to my bag of rocks.

The police asked me what I'd cut myself on, and when I told them that it was something down there in the dark that ripped at me and stole my brother, that officer looked to the ambulance driver and told him I was in shock.

Shock. Yeah, that was a word for it.

Another word or three, maybe even four, would be, "Scared to fucking death." See, it wasn't the fact that my momma had tied us down with rocks and dropped us in the river that had me terrified of the water for the rest of my eking life. It was because where she dropped us, there should have been only a few feet of water above our heads, but when I looked up, looked around, there was an ocean between us and anything else, and we were falling down, down, down, until no light broke the water that filled our lungs. Down, down, until the earth split, and something crawled right out of hell.

From then on, after I got washed up somehow on the bank, I could hear that siren call. When I sat next to the water on that ambulance trying to warm up and come to terms with where I saw my brother go, that high, piercing song from the deep bubbled up from the river and caressed my ears. Whenever I heard that song, though, all I could see was that blue light turn red as my brother's skin flapped free from his neck and arms – those gnarled, clawed hands digging in and ripping him through the void.

I heard them sing to me in the bath at the old lady's house – Margie, who'd become my surrogate mom. I don't know if she ever believed me about the singing or the things at the bottom of the river, but I stopped taking baths, and she'd help me in the shower just as quick as I could get clean. She couldn't let me go when she held me tight in that scratchy blanket against the river the day she found me, and when my mother was sentenced after what I told the courts, Margie and Ed adopted me as their own.

Ed passed when I was twelve, and Margie died alone in her bed when I was sixteen and a half. I found her there like that, naked, wrapped in a towel, bath still steaming and drawn in her bedside bathroom. Her eyes were open and this look of terror I'll never forget wrapped her face like it was painted on.

When I looked from her dead eyes to where they were turned to her bathroom, I saw my brother looking at me from the water. Half his head breached the surface, his hair running wet down his face. I couldn't see his mouth there under the water, under the edge of the tub, and I thanked god for that – but his eyes were a pale yellow like the sun got a sickness, and when he dipped back below, he was gone for good. I braved the edge of the tub and peered in, only to see nothing waiting for me there at all. No brother calling me home, despite the song that slowly faded as the bubbles that breached the surface died away.

I saw my brother a few more times over the years. Sometimes when I'd be forced to sit along the edge of the pool in gym in high school, the teachers excusing this because of my past, I would see him in the water. He looked the same as the night his visage had killed my adoptive mother – head half out of the water, hair streaming down his face, and his eyes just burning into mine with that sickly yellow, staring at me like it was me who put him there. Me who left him alone in the river.

Sometimes in my quick showers, I'd hear that angelic song start rising in tamber, and I'd feel eyes staring into the back of my head. When I'd turn around, there was never anything there, until there was.

But we'll get to that.

For the most part, it was just the song, and then the visions of my brother in the random spots of water I'd find myself at or around. Him and his reverent eyes, gazing through me, burning me right up.

One time I was doing the dishes when my washer broke, sink full of brown water and suds, and I felt hands grab at my wrist and try to pull me in. When I freed myself, I had these gashes down my arm, looking like I stuck my fist through a glass window or something.

That wasn't my brother, I knew. That was them. At least I hoped so.

There's something strange about avoiding death and knowing that you should have died. Like you escaped, but into what? Back into life? Back into these thoughts like you don't belong here, and that darkness you tempted is always stretching its fingers out to grip at you again. I always had this feeling like the ground was going to open below me wherever I was, that blue light spilling out, and those arms, scaled and gnarled, just prodding the air to rip me from the earth.

I don't know what that had to do with my brother, but on long lonely nights, I thought of filling the bathtub to conjure him up again. Just so I could talk to him if he'd even hear it. Tell him it wasn't my fault. That he could leave me alone now.

I never was that brave, though.

Hell, even on stormy nights, nights so blustering and blowing where the rain washes against your window like you're seeing your yard through a waterfall, I felt him there with me on the other side of the glass. If I peered for long, I'd catch him standing out there, a dark silhouette, with embers for eyes, burning right through the dark to scar me again.

When my mother died at the prison, I knew before even being told. I knew because I was tired and sore from working on the line at the shop, and I was soaking in the hottest shower of my life, steam so thick you could choke on it if you breathed deep enough. I must have drifted off just standing there because I didn't even hear the singing. I jumped, damn near slipped and killed myself when a cold and clammy hand fell upon my shoulder, and I wheeled around, and there she was.

My mother stood there in the shower with me, naked as the day she was born, her eyes these black pits, pinned by these rays of golden light, and in front of her, she clutched my big - my little brother by his shoulders, and they both reached for me with hands that didn't belong to them. Hands with jagged claws, dripping black muck that splattered against the porcelain tub..

I fell back, crashing through the curtain, getting wrapped up in the damn thing, and when I finally ripped it off, there was nobody there to see my shame. Nobody. And you might be saying to yourself, *oh, it's just the trauma.* Or, *this lady is simply crazy,* and I'll be honest, I thought those same things too for a time. But when I peered back over the ledge of that tub, that black, silty sludge that dripped from their hands was spiraling down my drain.

That was yesterday.

I got the call from the prison that my mom was dead. I asked how, and they told me it was an accident in the showers. I didn't need to pry any further - I knew. It made me sad then, made me feel that shame I was mentioning, that shame that I put her there in that prison without understanding what had happened.

That song had called to her, too.

Out there at the river's edge back then, back where we used to eat lunch sometimes and play in the water, water so shallow it only touched my bottom as a little girl. Something, whatever they were, had called to my momma then, and when she walked us into that water and dropped us down like discarded trash, she hadn't done that on her own free will.

She spent the rest of her life in that prison, like me, afraid of the water, and eventually it caught up to her, maybe mad at her broken promise. Mad I got away.

I knew then it was only a matter of time for me, and I had a lot of thoughts then too, that maybe if those creatures had gotten what they wanted from me back then, maybe my brother's soul would be at rest. Maybe my mother could finally be at peace. Maybe my head wouldn't suddenly fill with visions of the deep and the things that dwell there.

So I went back to that clearing – that boat launch by the river, still looking the same as the day I was supposed to die, and I waited there until the sky turned that sort of pink it does when you've had just about the best day before it's time to go inside and rest. When that pink finally scattered on the horizon, I looked out over the water, and there was my mother, all slim and fit and soaked from head to where her waist dipped into the water, and I could see she had her arms open like ready to embrace me in our final hug.

And you know, at first I was scared, because the closer I got to the water, the more her eyes glinted in the dying light of the sky, reflecting like a pike or an eel when the surface light flits through the water just right, and the more I could see of her that wasn't cast in shadow, the more I could see her for what she was becoming.

Then that song started up again. I shouldn't say song, because it's more of just singing, and it mostly feels like it's in your head, but like you conjured up into your thoughts just the most beautiful thing that could possibly exist in all the universe.

The cold slipped over my shoes and my socks squished around in there, and when the water wetted the knees of my pants, my little big brother surfaced next to my momma. She scooped him up and held him up by her shoulders, and they both looked to me with their arms held out, like ready to fold me into them and never let me go.

The scales on their arms glittered in the sunset, and the cool river water dripped in silent drops from their jagged claws. I felt the ground rumble beneath us, causing the surface of the water to ripple out in successive waves. The cold blue, like the color of dead flesh, opened beneath the water as my mother wrapped me in her arms.

CONTRIBUTORS

Bill Link is a lifelong resident of the Spokane/Spokane Valley area where most of his fiction takes place. He has published two novellas in the horror and weird fiction genre: *Skin Like Tanned Leather,* and *At Night Outside The Window,* as well as three anthologies of his short fiction, *Creeping Shadows, You're Always With Me And Other Stories,* and *Six Times The Terror.* He lives with his wife (and best friend), their daughter, and their cat, Lovecraft.

Nadim Silverman is a Bangladeshi-Jewish writer and illustrator based in New York City. He is currently studying creative writing at SUNY Stony Brook's MFA program. His work has been featured in *Flash Fiction Magazine, BULL, The After Happy Hour Review,* and more.

R.S. Morgan is an award-winning writer who has been publishing fiction and nonfiction nationally since 1983, when his work debuted in *Mike Shayne Mystery Magazine.* Most recently, in 2022, *Mystery Tribune* featured his surreal suspense. In 2021, *Black Cat Mystery Magazine* published his literary suspense and in 2020 Mystery Tribune published his crime fiction. In 2017, *Mystery Weekly Magazine* published his Wiccan suspense as its cover story. His nonfiction credits include feature articles for *Razor* and *Skiing.* He is also a retired UAW skilled tradesman and a retired first responder. His email is rsmorgan812@gmail.com.

Curt Tyler is a London writer of sci-fi, horror and satire. He plays guitar and cooks good curry.

Wayne Kyle Spitzer is an American writer, illustrator, and filmmaker. He is the author of countless books, stories and other works, including a film (*Shadows in the Garden*), a screenplay (*Algernon Blackwood's The Willows*), and a memoir (*X-Ray Rider*). His work has appeared in *MetaStellar—Speculative fiction and beyond, subTerrain Magazine: Strong Words for a Polite Nation* and *Columbia: The Magazine of Northwest History,* among others. He holds a Master of Fine Arts degree from Eastern Washington University, a B.A. from Gonzaga University, and an A.A.S. from Spokane Falls Community College. His recent fiction includes *The Man/Woman War* cycle of stories as well as the *Dinosaur Apocalypse Saga.* He lives with his sweetheart Ngoc Trinh Ho in the Spokane Valley.

David Sheskin is a writer and artist who has been published extensively over the years. Most recently his work has appeared in *The Los Angeles Review, Filling Station, Palooka, The Madison Review* and *Does It Have Pockets.* His most recent books are *David Sheskin's Cabinet of Curiosities* and *Outrageous Wedding Announcements.*

Meg Keane is a librarian & writer of speculative fiction and folk horror who has been published by *Creepy, Chilling Tales for Dark Nights, Black Sheep Magazine, Crow & Cross Keys, The Broken Spine, BMR Magazine, The Evermore Review* and more. She was also included in *Good For Her: A Celebration of Women's Wrongs* in 2024. Her nonfiction on her chronic illness can be found in *WellBeing Magazine.* Find her editing during witching hours or lurking in the shadows on X @megmkeane and Insta @megkeanewrites

Nathan Perrin (he/him/his) is a writer and Anabaptist pastor in Chicagoland. He holds an MA in Quaker Studies, and is a doctoral student studying Christian Community Development at Northern Seminary. His doctorate work centers on creating a writing program for nonprofits and churches to use to help under-resourced communities process trauma. His work has been published in the *Dillydoun Review, Bangalore Review, Collateral Journal, Esoterica Magazine,* etc. His forthcoming novella *Memories of Green Rivers* will be released in winter 2025 by Running Wild Press. He is also a screenwriter for an unannounced indie comedy series. For more information, visit www.nathanperrinwriter.com

Alexander Zelenyj is the author of the books *Blacker Against the Deep Dark, Songs for the Lost, Experiments at 3 Billion A.M., Black Sunshine,* and others. His most recent book is *These Long Teeth of the Night: The Best Short Stories 1999-2019.* His books and stories have been translated into several languages, including German, French, Romanian, Italian, Spanish, and Ukrainian. He has a collection of brand new stories forthcoming from Eibonvale Press in Fall 2024. Zelenyj lives in Windsor, Ontario, Canada with his wife and their growing menagerie of animals.

Dylan T. Bosworth (he/him) is a writer and enthusiast of all things dark and dreadful. He is most often found somewhere deep in the Midwest, teaching his two children how to survive the horrors of Small Town, America. In his free time, he obsessively reads and clacks away at the keyboard. When not scribbling or scrutinizing, he prefers playing chess and cooking.

Printed in Great Britain
by Amazon